JASON
AND·THE
ARGONAUTS

JASON
AND·THE
ARGONAUTS

BERNARD EVSLIN

ILLUSTRATED BY BERT DODSON

WILLIAM MORROW & COMPANY
NEW YORK

Library of Congress Cataloging-in-Publication Data
Evslin, Bernard.
Jason and the Argonauts.
Summary: Ekion, the son of Hermes, relates how he
came to be one of Jason's Argonauts and the adventures
they shared in search of the Golden Fleece.
1. Jason (Greek mythology)—Juvenile literature.
2. Argonauts (Greek mythology)—Juvenile literature.
[1. Jason (Greek mythology)   2. Mythology, Greek]
I. Title.
BL820.A8E95 1986   292'.13   85-32114
ISBN 0-688-06245-8

FOR OUR OWN NOAH, LOVER OF THE SURF . . .
MAGIC VOYAGES AND HAPPY LANDFALLS.

JASON
A N D · T H E
ARGONAUTS

O N E

THIS STORY BEGINS very soon after the world began, when great raw things called monsters roamed the unfinished places eating whatever they could catch. The earth was flat then, as anyone could tell; it had been broken into islands and the pieces flung upon a huge puddle of sea. The islands bobbed uneasily on the heaving purple water and had to be pinned down by mountains or they would have blown away altogether; that's how strong the winds were.

On top of one of these mountains, called Olympus, lived a family of gods. They had chosen Olympus because it was high enough to look down upon the pasture lands of the restless new herds they had inherited: strange, wild, and clever creatures, neither god nor beast but something in between, who called themselves men and women and were difficult to manage.

The gods loved to hunt and soon found that men and women, although lacking horns or claws and absurdly slow-footed, nevertheless offered fine sport, for human prey, unlike any other, kept trying to understand what was happening to them. But, try as they might, they could make no sense of these arrows that struck out of nowhere,

 1

taking the young and strong as well as the old and feeble. And their anguished confusion amused the gods mightily.

Finally, Zeus, the king of the gods, saw that the human herd was shrinking before the invisible arrows faster than it could replace itself, and he decided to lay down some game laws. It was forbidden to kill more than a certain small quota of humans each month, and the penalties were severe. He decreed that anyone who broke the new law would be chained to the roots of a mountain in Tartarus and kept there in suffocating darkness through eternity.

The gods feared Zeus. They knew how ferocious he could be when crossed. So they pretended to obey. But as time passed, they found a way to break the law without suffering the penalties.

They employed monsters—particularly dragons, who developed a taste for heroes.

And now that we know something about the games gods play, and the reason for dragons, we can better follow the adventures of those who shipped with Jason on his quest for the Golden Fleece.

T W O

EKION

LET'S START WITH ME, Ekion.

I am a son of Hermes by one of the Nymphs of the Grove, which one I'm not sure. Hermes married all three one summer night and planted a son in each. Consequently, we were all born on the same summer afternoon, and our mothers found it convenient to swap us around, giving one another more time to do what nymphs do. We were shifted around so much that the sisters forgot who had borne whom, and none of them ever cared whether it was a son or a nephew she was suckling at her breast.

But if we were unclear who was our mother and who were our aunts, we did know who our father was. Hermes visited the grove from time to time bringing a hot silver moonlight with him, always, and the music of pipe and lyre—which he had invented—and danced with the sisters all night long.

So there were the three boys: myself, Autolycus, and Daphnis. We'll get to them; they became Argonauts, too, but let's consider me first.

Let's take my name. Do you know what "Ekion" means in our language? It means "viper." *Viper.* Perhaps it began as a pet name.

The nymphs played rough—seizing us and tossing us from one to the other, tickling, biting, kissing us all over. Their speech could be wild and rough, too. But of the three I was the only one given an unkind name. "Daphnis" means "laurel." "Autolycus" means "wolfish," but in a noble sense. And I was called Ekion, a poisonous little snake, swift and deadly. What a name for an innocent child to bear. For I *was* innocent, until the age of two anyway.

Two brothers—I hated one and feared the other. Daphnis was chubby, clinging, clumsy in movement, and slow in speech, and everyone loved him best—except me. His eyes were like wet violets, and I wanted to poke them out with a sharp stick. Oddly enough, he was so cuddly and smelled so delicious that I liked to hug and kiss him, too, and disliked him more for confusing me.

The three of us were exactly the same age, as I told you, but anyone looking at us would have thought that Autolycus was two years older. He was a tall, sturdy boy with a brown-gold shock of hair thick as a pelt and a narrow fierce face. He had the quickest pair of hands anyone had ever seen; to fight him was madness. His fists were a blur, and he could blacken my eyes and bloody my nose before I could get in a blow. This was the reason Daphnis was more or less safe from me. Autolycus had appointed himself his protector and thrashed me every time I began to educate the little half-wit.

Those same fast hands later gave him his vocation. He became a master thief.

In Daphnis, feeble-mindedness turned lyrical: he became a poet.

Hermes seemed to find us entertaining. Upon one visit he gathered us about him and said, "Sons of the grove, I rejoice in the sight of you. For it is a sad fact that god spawn are not always godlike. Handsome Dionysus and gorgeous Aphrodite, for instance, did not breed true. They produced a misshapen little gargoyle called Priapus. But I have been luckier here in the grove. I see in each of you some expression of my godhead. I am Lord of Thieves, as you know—and you, Autolycus of the swift hands, shall raise larceny to an art. I am also he who invented the lyre, and so am associated with that sweet primal utterance called poetry—wherein speech partakes of song—and you, Daphnis, heaven help you, show symptoms of that vocation."

"Why must heaven help me, Da-da?" lisped Daphnis, making me want to kill him on the spot.

"Because, my son, poetry can be a cruel gift. A very mixed blessing. Nevertheless, I have bred true, and I am proud of you."

They were all looking at me now. I stood there waiting. Hermes didn't say anything. But I saw laughter smoldering in his gray eyes, tugging at the corner of his lips. He can read my heart and knows that I love him more than all the others put together, that I worship him, and it amuses him to tease me. He lolled there on the grass now, the silvery one, smiling that subtle smile.

I couldn't stand it any longer. "How about me, Father?"

"What about you?"

"What have I inherited?"

"What indeed, little viper?"

"Viper," I said slowly. "Yes-ss. Perhaps I am your true heir."

He threw back his head and chortled. "You are quick-witted, suave in manner, fancy of speech, with more taste for negotiation than combat. If you can but learn to smile when you want to kill, you might make a pretty fair herald. And I am also Patron of Heralds, you know."

"I've never thought of myself that way," I said.

"Fortunately, you have an affectionate father to do your thinking for you. Herald I have named you, and herald you shall be—a profession that will make you the confidant of kings and put you squarely in the middle of great events. A profession more profitable than theft, and less hazardous. A calling more comfortable in every way than that of poet. Your person shall be inviolate, you shall bear the sacred truce and most closely resemble me, Herald to the High Gods."

"I thank you, Father."

"Come kiss me."

I did. He sprang into the air, ankle wings whirring, and I didn't see him again until that fateful day when he first told us about Jason.

Of envy and hatred am I compounded.

The very glands under my jaw grow heavy with venom. My teeth grow hollow for it; my body dwindles and moves in stealth when I think of that Jason whom my father called the most beautiful boy on this disk of earth.

THREE

JASON'S TROUBLES BEGAN when he was still a baby, on the day that his father, Diomedes II, suddenly stopped being king of Iolcus. The king was a gentle man, still young, and would have reigned many more years if it had not been for his stepbrother, Pelius the Impatient. He knocked Diomedes on the head and rolled him off a cliff into the sea, then named himself regent because the crown prince was an infant.

Pelius's first royal act was to declare war on a neighboring country to give people something else to think about. Because he had plans for his nephew. He meant to solve the problem of succession very simply by dropping the baby out the window. But when he went to the nursery that night, he found the crib empty. He was frantic. He ordered the palace turned inside out. Every cottage, barn, and haystack for miles around was searched and searched again, but the infant prince had been swallowed by the night.

Thereupon Pelius announced that, in the light of the royal baby's disappearance, it was the clear duty of the regent, who happened to be himself, to choose a new king, also himself. And now, as king, he could get on with the business of winning the war and celebrating that victory with another war, and on and on, until every patriotic Iolchian would thank the gods for allowing them to be ruled by a winner, even if he had been lethal about gaining the throne.

Pelius prospered. He grew in fame and wealth, getting meaner and fatter each year. But even as paunch and power grew, he kept being haunted by the idea that the little prince was alive somewhere and would turn up one day to claim his kingdom. He gave orders that every young stranger in the kingdom was to be watched very closely and killed on the spot if he came within ten miles of the castle.

F O U R

ZEUS HAD A BROTHER named Hades who ruled the dead. Tartarus was his kingdom, an underground realm of linked caverns where the homeless spirits were taken after being evicted from their bodies.

Squeaking and gibbering, each day's draft of fresh ghosts were herded through vast, shifting shadows toward the Place of Judgment. Invisible hands seized them; they were made to shuffle past a throne of ebony and pearl, where sat Hades—huge, black-robed, silent. With one glance he judged each spirit, and with a flick of his hand he sent it off to be indulged, ignored, or tormented through eternity.

Upon this day, Hades was in a bad temper and sent more than the usual number of souls to the roasting pits. Nor did he arise from his throne after the last whimpering shade had been whisked away, but sat there waiting. Earlier that day he had sent for Ares and had been told that the god of war was on his way.

Ares strode into the throne room. He was the largest of the gods, who are all huge. He wore a breastplate, shin greaves, and helmet, all of brass. Crossing the floor, he absorbed every bit of light in that gloomy chamber. He burned upon the shadows. His great arms were hard as marble; his face was a slab of raw beef. His eyes were pits of redness.

Hades descended from his throne and embraced Ares; it was like black sleeves of smoke winding about a fire.

"Lord of Battles, I greet you."

"All reverence, my melancholy master," said Ares. "How can I serve you?"

"Are you acquainted with Jason, prince of Iolcus?"

"No, sire, I am not."

"I desire you to make his acquaintance," said Hades.

"I take it he is someone you dislike?"

"Someone I loathe. Very young, but growing into a first-class troublemaker."

"How can a puny mortal trouble *you*, Lord of Darkness?"

"It has been foretold that he shall father a child who shall possess an uncanny talent for healing, thus depriving me of my rightful quota of corpses."

"You can't always believe these things. Prophets are gloomy by nature; maybe it won't happen."

"The warning cannot be doubted. It is written on the Scroll."

What he meant was this: every so often, those twisted sisters called the Fates, whom even the gods fear, would dip their claws into starlight and scrawl their decrees upon a great scroll. Night blue was the Scroll; it hung from a place in the heavens beyond man's sight and was written upon in letters of fire. Once every several years the gods were summoned to read the Scroll and to consider how to use their divine powers within these laws.

"On the Scroll were the dreadful words written," said Hades. "I must neither doubt them nor ignore them. And, indeed, this accursed young prince has himself displayed dangerous healing power, only on animals so far, but the tendency is there. Just this year he was able to stop a cattle plague, which has made him beloved among the herdsmen of Cythera. So, my nephew, it falls upon us to overturn this prophecy."

"How can you alter a decree of the Fates?" asked Ares. "As it is written, so must it be."

"The way the sentence reads, I have room to maneuver," said Hades. "It says, 'If this youth becomes a man and fathers a child, that child shall be a great healer.' It is my intention to cut his career short before he becomes a father."

"Did he really cleanse cattle of the plague?" asked Ares, who owned vast herds.

"He did. And the people dubbed him 'Jason,' which in their dialect means 'healer.' I'd like him killed. Will you do it?"

"Forgive me, good Uncle. But my game bag is overfull, and I hesitate to break the law."

"You should know more about this young man. He is of the type of Adonis."

"What do you mean?" whispered Ares.

"Slender, ivory-limbed, gray-eyed—the type that Aphrodite favors. In fact, knowing him in danger, she has set a Thessalian witch to hover over the island, keeping ceaseless vigil."

At the very sound of the name Adonis, Ares had begun to swell with rage. His neck and face went dusky red, his teeth shone, his eyes bulged. He looked like a wild boar. And indeed it was in the shape of a wild boar that he had attacked young Adonis some years before and trampled him into bloody rags. Since that time, no one had dared approach Aphrodite.

"Favors him, does she?" he panted. "And does she visit the island?"

"Not yet," said Hades. "I fancy she considers him too young. But she must have plans in that direction, or why would she employ a witch to watch over him?"

"Yes-ss, Aphrodite always has a reason for what she does, and it's always the same. Too young, is he? Well, I'll see that he doesn't get any older."

"Good . . . good."

"How about that witch? She can't stop me, but she can raise an alarm."

"She won't see you. She'll be busy." Hades then put his lips to Ares' ear, and whispered.

Ares bellowed with laughter. "That should hold the old bag!"

"Good hunting."

"I'll bring you his head."

F I V E

ACOLD WIND BLEW OVER the slopes of Olympus. Aphrodite walked out of the garden and into the orchard. The pomegranate trees were being stripped by the wind, and the fig trees and the wild olives. But standing green among the fruit trees were fir and spruce and pine. Snow began to sift. Olympus stands in northern Thessaly; it is capped by snow from autumn till spring. It was autumn now. She was barefoot, clad in a blue tunic. Her throat was bare, and her shoulders and her long white arms.

A bright yell split the air—Hermes' herald call. He flashed like a blade, catching all the dull light. She watched as he fell toward her, his face drinking light.

He saw her among trees in the cold green dusk, growing taller and taller as he coasted down steeps of air into the clean smell of pine.

He came to her. He saw snow melting about her feet and roses springing where she stood.

"You sent for me, O beautiful one?"

"I need your help."

"Queen of the Night, whatever is in my power I shall perform."

"I have chosen again among mortals."

"Let me guess the rest. You want my assistance in defending him against the jealous gods."

"He is startlingly like Adonis. Not surprising: he is also descended from Io."

"Therefore, perhaps, one of my own descendants," murmured Hermes.

"Quite possibly, dear friend. He is Jason, exiled prince of Iolcus, dwelling now upon the island of Cythera."

"Does Ares know about him?"

"I don't see how he could. I don't visit the island. Not yet."

"Well, if Ares doesn't know . . . "

"In that brawling bully, jealousy becomes insight. He has an uncanny way of sniffing out my favorites. But I shall not permit Jason to meet the doom of Adonis."

"And what do you expect me to do—go to battle with the god of war? Do you really think that I, the most fragile and least bellicose of the Olympians, can stop that murderous brute in the full spate of his wrath?"

"I'm not asking you to fight him. I need your wits, not your sword. As I say, I don't know that he's even aware of Jason's existence, but I would like you to fly over the island. Just look things over, make sure my sentinel witch is being vigilant or see if I shall have to take stronger measures."

"I don't relish this chore, but I can refuse you nothing."

"You'll find me grateful."

S I X

THE HAG HUNG IN THE AIR over Cythera, gathering her cloak about her until she looked like a huge black crow. She carted a leather sack in which she had sewn up a patch of fog. When she saw anyone approaching, she would swoop down to the treetops, ripping open her sack as she dived, and swiftly crisscross the island, laying a ground fog. And no one flying above could see through the rolling mist. When the danger had passed, the witch would roll up her fog and stuff it back in the bag. She was eager to serve Aphrodite, for she was a ravenously greedy old crone, and the goddess had promised an endless supply of her favorite food if she kept the boy safe.

It was roast piglet she craved. And when her tour of duty was done, Aphrodite had told her, she would be furnished with a sow out of the Olympic sty itself. These sows were magical, littering daily and supplying the delicate suckling pork that graced the gods' own table.

Disguised as a gull, Hermes was flying over Cythera. He spotted a hunched black shape coasting along beneath him and slanted down.

Witches did not ride broomsticks then. They rode bats, rats—vultures sometimes, but these were unreliable, diving suddenly when they saw a corpse. In fact, an experienced witch could make any creature fly like a bird by rubbing it with a certain magic ointment. This witch rode a snake. It was a Libyan anaconda, twelve feet long, and as thick as the anchor cable for a Phoenician warship. It was as loyal as a dog, was tireless in flight, and ate goats.

Hermes watched the witch riding her snake. She was flying low, just skimming the treetops. Effortlessly, on gull wings, he coasted the bright slopes of air, keeping near the witch as she crisscrossed the island. She seemed to examine every bush, every tree, every shadow. Having assured himself of her industry and vigilance, Hermes angled off and flew his own course, searching for Jason—whom he had never seen.

Finally he saw a boy running along the strip of beach that divided sea from forest. The runner was naked except for a quiver of arrows. Hermes couldn't see his face; all he saw were slender flashing legs and floating black hair. The boy moved like a blown leaf, plucking an arrow from his quiver as he ran, notching it, bending his bow, and launching the shaft—all in one swift, fluid motion, without ever breaking stride. His first arrow struck a cypress tree, the second arrow split the first one, and every arrow after that split the one that preceded it. Hermes, who had invented the bow and trained generations of demigod bowmen, had never seen archery to equal this.

It was low tide, and Hermes spotted dark shapes lurking in a tidal pool. The shapes broke water as the boy ran past, revealing themselves as two bronzed nereids with green hair. Shrieking with laughter, the lithe sea nymphs flung themselves upon the lad. The three figures tumbled upon the sand and crawled over one another like a litter of puppies. The nereids clutched at Jason, tickling him and competing to see who could kiss more of him. He tried to fend them off, but he was weak with laughter.

The witch dived, screaming. She swooped down upon the tangle, sliding toward the snake's head and making it pivot in the air and crack its tail like a bullwhip. It flailed at the nereids, flogging them away from Jason, then following them. The witch rode astride, screaming, as the snake flew backward, lashing the nereids, who were weeping now as they fled toward the sea, their backs striping with great red weals under the live whip.

They dived into the waves. The witch rode back, cackling at Jason, who turned from her without speaking. Obviously he loathed his chaperone. The witch flew her snake along the sand, making sure the nereids would not reappear. She circled Jason a few times, who was now sitting moodily on the beach, drawing hideous witch faces on the sand with a stick. Then she flew off.

Hermes landed on the beach as gulls do and walked stiff-legged toward the boy. He stopped near and studied him. Jason lounged there, idly scratching a stick in the wet sand. One leg was curled, the other straight; his back was bent. And the angles and curves and straight planes of his body flowed into each other, harmonizing without artifice like a half-grown panther's, like the visual equivalent of music. He raised his face and stared out to sea. His eyes were a color rarely seen, a pale pure gray, darkening now like pieces of sky as they grew stormy with thought.

"I have invented the bow, the fire stick, the pipes, and the lyre," said Hermes to himself. "Also weights and measures, money, and astronomy. Of all my creations, though, I am proudest of this beautiful boy, my great-great-great-grandson through beloved Io. I understand Aphrodite's madness and her fear. Such beauty is fatal to its possessor."

Light splintered faintly in the far northern reaches of the sky. As Hermes watched, a ball of light grew there and rolled toward them, getting larger as it came. Hermes spread his gull wings and flew up to investigate. He coasted the currents of air over the island, watching. It was not a ball of fire but points of light bunching, trundling. He heard a golden bugling sound as of great stallions trumpeting.

And now he saw what was coming: Ares' brass chariot pulled by great roan stallions across the blue meadow of the sky—wheel spokes flashing, hub-knives turning and casting sheaves of light. Ares stood tall at the reins, helmet and breastplate flashing.

"Can he be doing it so crudely?" thought Hermes. "Simply charging across the sky in full daylight to murder the boy?"

He flew higher, angling away from the island, placing himself above the path of the oncoming chariot. He saw a black smudge shooting out from behind the treetops. It was the witch on her snake, climbing to intercept the chariot.

"I shall hover here and watch her in action," he said to himself. "I'm eager to see her lay her ground fog and watch that brass bully groping through the magic mist."

She had climbed now to a spot just below Hermes and floated there as the chariot grew larger and larger, thundering toward her. She reached into her pouch. Then Hermes saw her head snap about as if something below had caught her attention. He looked down and saw something floating in the sea. A plume of smoke arose. Gulls swooped toward the smoke. Hermes was another gull diving.

It was a raft floating there, but weirdly freighted. It bore a platform of stones; on that platform a fire burned. Tending the flame was one of Hades' turnspit demons, and turning on the spit was a suckling pig, its skin crackling, sending rich savors into the air that maddened the gulls.

The witch stuffed the scroll of fog back into her pouch and put her snake into a dive. She plunged toward the water, shrieking gleefully, scattering the gulls. They rose, screaming back at her in the path of her dive.

"A decoy!" thought Hermes. "This is no brute assault but a coordinated attack. They have drawn off the sentinel. Now Ares can kill Jason at his leisure."

The roan stallions were galloping under him now, pulling the great clattering brass chariot. Ares held the reins in one huge hand and a battle-ax in the other. Master charioteer that he was, he did not dive the horses toward the island with the tremendous weight of metal behind them, but brought them down along a gentle slope of descent.

Hermes also dived, became a bolt of gray feathers, and landed on the beach before Ares arrived. Jason was gone.

"I hope he has sense enough to hide in the wood," thought Hermes.

Ares' chariot landed on the beach. The stallions raced along the edge of the sea, trumpeting, rejoicing to feel the earth under their hooves again. Hermes rose into the air and followed the chariot as it made a complete circuit of the island.

"Jason!" roared Ares. "Jason! Where are you, you little rat? Coward! Are you prince or slave? Do you skulk in the woods when an enemy comes? Jason . . . Jason . . . come out and fight!"

Ares dismounted. The stallions pawed the earth, tossing their manes, rolling their brilliant eyes. Ares entered the woods, shouting, "Hide yourself well! Dig your hole deep, you dog! I'll dig you out wherever you are!"

"I'd better take a hand," said Hermes to himself. "Jason will never withstand these taunts. He's not hiding; I know he's not. He is couched on a limb like a young leopard waiting to spring on Ares as he passes beneath. For I know him, know him after just one look at him, know him right down to the lining of his heart. He will not wait in ambush like a seasoned warrior. No, he will seek to engage this killer hand to hand. I shall have to intervene."

He changed back into his own form and followed Ares into the woods. He could hear the war god ahead of him, trampling through the brush, shouting. Hermes broke into a smooth run, picking his way among the trees. He came so close that he heard Ares, no longer shouting, but speaking in a conversational way.

"I know you're near. I can smell you. I can always smell an enemy, especially a putrid cur like you. Stay there, lover boy. Stand and fight."

Then Hermes heard another sound, the sibilant whisper of arrow flight . . . heard Ares' voice raised again in an anguished bellow . . . heard the clanging of metal. He raced through a fringe of trees on the edge of a clearing and stopped short at the sight.

Ares stood in the clearing, brandishing his ax, bellowing, in the midst of an arrow swarm. It was as if the arrows were alive and were flying at him like giant wasps. The archer was invisible. Each arrow hit its mark—never touching Ares' flesh, never even scratching him, but finding the buckle point of each piece of armor and shearing it off him as neatly as a groom unharnessing a horse.

His breastplate dropped off, then his shin greaves. An arrow knocked his helmet askew, denting it. He tore it off his head with a wild bellow. Now he stood there, hulking and hairy as a bear, but bigger than any bear. A last arrow sang out of the thicket and hit his crotch guard, making it ring like a bell. Ares doubled up in pain.

Hermes saw Jason step out into the clearing. He had been expecting this, but the actual appearance of the boy struck him like a fist under the heart. Jason was naked, unarmed except for a hunting knife. He was slender as a peeled wand, his eyes like pieces of ice under his dark brows.

Ares held his battle-ax. Its haft was a young tree, its head larger

🌿 21 🌿

than Jason's body and honed to a razor edge. Others had tried to use this ax—gods, demigods, titans, giants—but Ares was the only one strong enough. He not only used it to strike with, but hurled it like a hatchet. Hermes had seen him behead a giant at fifty paces. If he missed a throw, the ax would circle back to his hand, and he would be ready to throw again.

All this flashed through Hermes' mind in the wink of an eye. The silvery messenger god stood, in a trance, watching the lad glide across the clearing, as if courage by some foul twist had been converted into fatal trust, making the beautiful boy offer his throat to the butcher's blade. Slowly Ares raised his ax.

Hermes changed himself into a woodpecker—but a giant one, bigger than an eagle, with an iron beak. He flew to a tree at the edge of the clearing, a towering pine, clutched himself to the trunk, and drove his iron beak into the bole. He pulled it out and struck again, and again and again, his head moving faster than a hummingbird's. He moved around the trunk, driving his beak in again and again, working so fast that, before Ares had finished poising his ax, he was hit by the falling tree. He was smashed to earth and buried among the branches.

Jason stood there, bewildered. Hermes returned to his own form. He came up behind the boy and touched him with his herald staff, casting him into a deep sleep. He caught the boy in his arms and flew away, climbing swiftly past the treetops. He bore him to the other side of the island and laid him in the shade of a tree, still asleep.

He knelt there, staring at the sleeper, then he lightly kissed his face and flew back to where Ares lay, but did not linger. Already the pine branches were threshing as the fallen god strove to rise.

Hermes flew eastward. He saw something that made him swoop. The witch rode the raft. She was gurgling and jigging and gnawing a pork bone. The fire was out. The turnspit demon was asleep. From time to time the hag wiped her hands on his curly pate. Hermes hovered, watching—but the witch, who noticed everything, was so busy eating that she did not see the god shining above her head. The sleeper snored. She screamed and frothed, epileptic with pleasure.

Hermes climbed again and flew away from the great burning ball of the setting sun.

S E V E N

EKION

I WAS WATCHING THE SKY for my father. He had sent no word, but I knew he was coming. I saw a splinter of light, then a streak of fire. He landed among us, pot-shaped hat pulled over his eyes, twirling his staff until the twined snakes seemed alive. And I thought my heart would burst with pride when he unwound Daphnis' arm from around his neck and motioned to me.

"I need your help."

I couldn't say anything. I just looked at him. He smiled.

"I'm sending you away."

"Far?"

"You'll be seeing more of me than ever."

"Oh, Father . . . "

"You will go to the court of Iolcus and take employment with King Pelius."

"As herald?"

"His herald, my spy."

"What's he like?"

"A tyrant, a glutton, a murderer. Not too different from most kings, but a bit more so."

I nodded, imitating composure.

"He may not sound like an ideal employer, but you'll be all right. Heralds are protected by sacred law. You will attend his councils, learn his plans, and tell me what he intends."

"I would know your own purpose, sire. Not from curiosity, but that I may serve you with more intelligence."

"Hearken, then. Pelius is a usurper. Some years ago he killed his stepbrother, who was the rightful king, and since then has been hunting his brother's son. That son, who is called Jason, is hidden on the island of Cythera. I have just visited this island. I went there at the request of Aphrodite, who has developed a passionate interest in the lad and fears for his safety."

"Surely a goddess can protect her paramour?"

"To contend against Ares you need allies. He will permit no rival and has a way of erasing her lovers before she can enjoy them. Indeed, I happened to arrive at the island just as he landed there."

"Did he kill the boy?" I asked, hoping he had.

"It was wonderful," he said. "Jason defied the war god and fought so gallantly, so skillfully, I didn't believe what I was seeing. He moves like light over water. He filled the air with arrows. Each found its mark and sheared off a piece of Ares' armor until he stood naked as a flayed steer."

"Vanquished Ares, did he?"

"Well, not quite. Ares is Ares, after all. But I was able to intervene, and it ended in a draw, more or less."

Each of his words were like one of those arrows piercing me. "So you left the brave young prince on his island?"

"I did."

"You didn't speak with him?"

"No."

"What exactly do you want me to do?"

"You must understand, son, that Diomedes III, now called Jason, has incurred the wrath of two expert architects of doom, namely, Hades and Ares. You should also be aware that, under the law of Zeus, gods can no longer kill mortals with their old freedom. But the Lord of Tartarus and the Lord of Battles have many resources. They can employ mortals to do their killing for them. Or monsters. Their next move may well involve Pelius, who is Jason's natural enemy and has an army and a battle fleet at his disposal. This is where I want your help. You shall keep me informed about what Pelius means to do—and, of course, hold yourself ready to help Jason in any way you can."

"Yes," I murmured, trying not to hiss. "I look forward to making Jason's acquaintance."

"To know him is to love him," said Hermes. "And to serve him is to please me."

"And to please you, Father, is my dearest wish."

E I G H T

EKION

PELIUS SPRAWLED ON HIS THRONE, sucking at his teeth. He did this when he was hungry, and he was always hungry. He'd grown so fat he couldn't see his feet; it made him wheeze and pant just to climb the three steps to his throne.

For the past few days he had been in an ugly mood. An oracle had told him that an enemy was coming. I tried to explain to him that all kings always had an enemy somewhere preparing to attack, and that oracles made a living out of such foolproof prophecies. But he didn't believe me. He chose to believe that someone was preparing an assault, and that this someone was Jason.

So we at court were having a difficult time. When the king was unhappy, he liked to share his pain, and for the past days he had signed so many death warrants that he had sprained his wrist and had to shift to his left hand. Every time I turned around suddenly, I saw him glaring at me, thinking how much better I'd look without a head.

His baleful glare was becoming unbearable to me, and the muffled terror of the courtiers had become thick as a stench in the gloomy throne room. I melted into the deepest shadow and slid out the great brass door without anyone noticing.

I went looking for a lad I knew, an apprentice smith named Rufus because of his red hair and fiery eyebrows. There was a Hephaestus cult in the country. The metal workers of Iolcus worshipped the smith-god and were considered priests. So the apprentice, Rufus, was not a slave but a novice and worked harder than a slave. He was a blunt, simple-hearted lad, the closest thing to a friend I had.

I scouted around the courtyard of the sacred smithy, but he didn't come out and I couldn't linger. So I set off alone. I missed my brothers more than I'd ever thought I would. I missed my mother, whichever sister she was, and my beautiful aunts. And Hermes hadn't come to see me.

But it was so good getting off among the trees and gliding through the fretted sunlight that I forgot about being lonesome and being prudent. I raced through a glade, leaping logs. I shouted and sang. I found a hollow tree and searched it for honeycombs, half hoping a bear would come and try to catch me as I fled. It was the kind of day on which your life changes forever and you can feel the change coming.

I reached a clearing. It was cut by a little stream, swollen now because the rains had been heavy these past weeks. The damp pine needles were steaming faintly, casting a maddening fragrance. My staff twitched in my hand. The snake that entwined it raised its carved head and spoke. Its voice was a silky whisper.

"Take leaves from that laurel tree. Cast them upon flame and breathe the smoke."

"Why?"

"It is your father's wish. You must enter trance and await his instructions."

I am not submissive by nature, but neither was I prepared to challenge anything a wooden snake said. A laurel tree stood at the edge of the clearing. I plucked a handful of its leaves, built a fire, and cast the leaves upon it. I knelt to the flame, inhaling its smoke. Darkness swarmed.

I stood at an oak stump, which was full of rainwater. A small wind blew, riffling the water. It was a miniature sea holding a ship as small as a walnut shell, its sail spread on a splinter of mast as it slid toward an oak-chip island.

Two huge rocks appeared. They stood apart from each other; the steersman put his bow exactly between them. But with an odd rushing, gurgling sound the boulders began to hurtle through the water toward each other. The ship slowed. I saw oars bend as the men tried to backwater—too slowly. The rocks were going with terrific speed now. They sluiced through the water and came together, crushing the tiny ship to splinters. I heard a frightful thin screaming, and the water grew red as I watched. The rocks sank, sucking the wreckage under. The stump sea was clear again.

It became a dish of molten silver in the hot sun. Pictures formed in its depths, floated up, and re-formed into something else: a bloody discus flying; a pair of hands cut off at the wrists, crawling like crabs; a pair of brass bulls breathing flame; a giant serpent with a man in its jaws.

I had left the stump. I sat near the fire, gazing into its heart. It was the sky burning. Under it lay scorched fields. Men and women lay there with blackened faces. Cattle that were racks of bone stood shakily, trying to snuffle something out of a dry riverbed. They lowed piteously and sank to earth. The sky burned. But now there was a golden core to the flame. It became a golden throne standing in the scorched field. On the throne sat a youth. He wore a gold crown. About his shoulders hung a great fleece, as if the pelt of a golden ram had been cut into a king's robe.

The young king raised his arms to the sky, and it darkened. The red flame became black smoke; the smoke whorled into storm clouds, and it all turned to rain. Water fell on the king and on his throne and on the parched earth The riverbeds filled, and the earth was green again. Then it all faded.

I spoke to the wooden snake. "What does my father wish?"

"Go fetch Jason. It's time."

"Time for what?"

"For him to learn what you have learned."

"Will he believe me?"

"Instruct him through vision. Harrow his sleep. Sow a dream."

The snake stiffened and twined woodenly about my staff. I was sitting over the ashes of the fire, and the day was hot and damp and still. I wanted to go to sleep, but it was time to be about my father's business.

N I N E

🌿 E K I O N

THE AIM OF DREAM-TINKERING is to frighten or flatter or otherwise persuade someone to do something by sowing certain visions in his sleeping head. There are two steps: first you cast the person into a swoon; then, when the eyes close and shallow breathing signifies deep trance, you begin to plant your dream.

Now I went about gathering the things I would need: a handful of laurel leaves; flower of poppy and mandragora and other slumberous herbs; some sprigs of withered barley; some shavings of ram's horn; and six boarlike bristles from the beard of Pelius.

I loaded my pouch with this potent rubbish and headed for the edge of the forest where it ran down to the sea.

Two days later, I was in Cythera. I stood at the foot of a cliff, looking up, up, trying to see who was standing on the edge. Whoever it was, he couldn't dive from that height; nobody could. Suddenly he dropped off.

I watched him fall. The sun caught him, body arched, arms spread. Did he realize he was plunging toward a sea full of rocks? They stood

🌿 32 🌿

thickly in the tide, the water boiling among them. He flashed down, his arms forward now, hair whipping backward in the wind of his going. He entered the water cleanly, splitting a tiny space between two rocks.

I watched for him to surface. Finally he did—closer to shore. He waded in. I knew he had to be Jason. My father had wrung my heart, describing his beauty.

"Greetings," he said.

"Greetings, Jason. I am Ekion, a herald by trade. May I know why you choose such a dreadful patch of sea?"

"Best place for diving."

"With those rocks?"

"You see, this is the highest cliff. The farther I fall, the more it is like flying."

"Speaking of that, where's your flying nursemaid? I heard tales of a hag on a snake?"

"She doesn't actually fly herself, you see, but astride an anaconda. Well, he's as greedy as she is and ate a goat without peeling it. So she's off to Libya to get another."

"Choked on a horn, did he?"

"Yes, poor thing. I couldn't pull it out. But, you know, it's ridiculous that we can't fly. Don't you agree? The stupidest birds can. And ugly old witches. All sorts of bugs. But not us."

"My father can."

He stared at me silently.

"Don't you believe me?"

"Does he have wings?"

"Ankle wings. *Talaria*, they're called."

"Where did he get them?"

"Always had them. He's a god. Hermes."

"Does he wear a pot-shaped hat?"

"He does."

"Carry a staff like yours?"

"Yes."

"You know, I was in a fight and got knocked on the head. And as I lay there, it seemed that this silvery god lifted me into the air and flew me to the other side of the island. Does he take you flying?"

"All the time." I had to hate him. My father never took me flying.

"Tell more lies," he said.

"I won't tell you anything if you call me a liar."

"Prove it's the truth. Make your father lend you his ankle wings, then lend them to me." He put his hand on my shoulder. His touch burned down to the bone. He smiled into my face. His eyes were like molten silver. His whole face became a blur of brightness. The bronze shield of his chest was burnished with light. I moved away. "Well," he said. "Shall we journey to Olympus and visit your lord father, and ask him to lend us his wings? Or will he come to us if you call?"

"He has taught me a few things," I said. "I can cast you into a sleep and make you dream you're flying. A vivid dream, almost like the real thing."

"I don't like almosts. I like more thans."

"Don't belittle what you have not known. It is of the gods, this visionary flight. Perhaps it is their way of teaching."

He stared at me. Oh, it was painful to meet the fierce purity of that gaze.

"Come, little herald," he said softly. "Do your trick."

I made a fire of twigs and sat him beside it. I dropped my handful of slumberous herbs into the flame and fanned the thin smoke toward him. His eyes closed.

I took the shavings of ram's horn from my pouch and dropped them on the fire. The pale flames turned gold and twisted themselves into horns. Jason muttered, uttered a strangled laugh. He was smiling as he slept.

After a bit, I took the sprigs of withered barley and threw them on the fire. The horns of flame dwindled, turned red, and burned sullenly. Jason moaned and trembled. I let him stew in the bitter lees of the vision, then emptied my pouch on the fire, dropping in the six bristles from the beard of Pelius.

The sleeper was angry now. His brows were knotted, his fingers scrabbling at the earth. He shouted something. I saw his eyelids quivering. I dipped water from the stream and doused the fire.

He opened his eyes, blinked, rubbed his head, spat. Then he flowed to his feet and crossed the clearing to the stream. He knelt and drank huge gulps. He plunged his head in, pulled it out, dripping. He glared at me.

"Who are you?"

"Still me. Ekion."

"Why have you come?"

"To plant a dream."

"It was a vision of horror. There was a drought on the land. Nothing green anywhere. People dying of thirst. And children and animals. Why did you make me dream that?"

"To show you what is to be. A drought is coming. The land shall sicken, its juices dry. Animals shall parch and die, wild animals and herds of cattle. And so people shall starve."

"When is this to happen?"

"That depends on you."

"On me?"

"You are a healer; you push back the hour of death."

"I can't cure a drought."

"Your dream showed you to yourself as rainmaker also."

"Who are you?"

"Perhaps I'm part of your dream?"

"No, I'm awake. You're real."

"The threat of drought is real, too. And it is your own kingdom that shall be worst stricken."

"My kingdom?"

"You know, do you not, that you are the rightful king of Iolcus?"

"So I have been told."

"You don't believe it?"

"Kings rule. Do I?"

"Hearken, Prince, your life is about to change. I have been sent to you. You are to come back to the mainland. You shall save your land from drought and your people from starvation. You shall overcome your enemies and reclaim your throne."

"I don't have the slightest idea how to do any of these things."

"All you have to do is the first thing; the rest will follow."

"What is the first thing?"

"To make rain."

"That's all, eh?"

"Rainmaking on a royal scale, cousin. Not just whistling up a few showers, or clacking the thunder bones for a season's moisture. I mean possessing yourself of a powerful magic that will bind the moon and swing the tides and roll up thirsty clouds to suck up the sea and spew it out as sweet abundant rain. I mean that you shall sit upon the throne of Iolcus wearing the pelt of the great golden ram— in whose fleece abides the strength to overturn the fountains of heaven and make the parched earth turn green, year after year after year."

"You did manipulate my vision. I rode a great golden ram. He had no wings but galloped through the air. The sky was purple-black, and there was lightning and thunder."

"That vision is a message from the gods and a call to action."

"Do you speak for the gods?"

"I have been sent to make their will known. You must come to Iolcus."

"How did you get here?" asked Jason.

"Waist-deep in squid. I hired a fishing smack."

"Send it back for me in three days."

T E N

EKION

THE KING WADDLED INTO THE council chamber, brimming with glee. He informed us that a young stranger had been captured on the northern shore and had calmly introduced himself to the spearmen as Diomedes III, otherwise known as Jason, their rightful king. Then Pelius told us what he meant to do with the prisoner.

Now, Pelius had simplified his penal system by abolishing trials. Accusation meant guilt; guilt meant death. Some few escaped beheading—those whom the king especially disliked and whom he wished to use for demonstrating the consequences of royal disfavor. These unlucky ones were locked in a wheeled cage that was dragged from village to village. Spectators were encouraged to prod the caged wretches with long poles, throw lighted torches through the bars, and otherwise torment them. But the ordeal didn't last long; no one survived more than a few days in a cage.

And it was into a cage that Jason was to go, the king informed us. If he happened to last more than a week, he was to be beheaded, his head stuck on a pole and paraded through the villages he had not visited.

The courtiers cheered and applauded. The king dismissed the council, bidding me stay. I stood before him as he overflowed the massive wooden throne that was his council seat.

"You were silent while the others were cheering," he said. "Do you dare to disapprove?"

"Zeal in your service, O King, outweighs any thought of risk."

"Bah—just what do you disapprove of?"

"You mean to exhibit this prince to the populace, which may well excite the very ideas you seek to discourage."

"How so?"

"This youth is some hundred pounds lighter than the ideal king should be, perhaps, and altogether lacks the majestic presence exhibited by Your Majesty. Nevertheless, we must never underestimate popular taste. There may be those who will be moved by the sight of him."

"What are you saying—they'll think he's good-looking?"

"Possibly . . . particularly women, who are more prone to frivolous judgment in such matters, and who are more passionate trouble-makers when aroused."

"Will you stop talking in that serpentine way, and tell me straight. You are saying it's a bad idea to cart him around in a cage because he may stir up sympathy?"

"A masterful conclusion, my lord."

"So what shall I do with him—just lop off his head?"

"If I may venture to suggest, I would do nothing until tomorrow."

"Why tomorrow? Why not today?"

"The gods who test a king with difficult choices also invest him with the wit to choose. Very often the gods reveal their will to the kings of earth by sending those night visions called dreams. As a son of Hermes, I have been given special insight into these matters and hereby predict that this very night you will be sent such a dream."

"Till tomorrow, then, and it may be your last morrow if you're as wrong as I think you are."

"Sleep soft, Your Majesty."

That night I slithered into the king's chamber.

A torch burned in a sconce on the wall, for the king feared assassins. I merged with the shadows. I dusted dry herbs into the torch flame and fanned the aromatic smoke toward the bed. His huge bulk quivered. He flung out an arm, gritted his teeth, mumbled wetly.

I slipped out and went to my own bed.

In the morning, a page summoned me to the royal garden. The king sat on a bench looking unusually yellow; his eyes were pouched in sagging flesh.

He said, "I had a dream all right, but I don't know its meaning."

"Shall I try to find one?"

"I don't want to talk about it."

"That would make interpretation difficult."

"It's too disgusting."

"In these readings, my lord, every detail is significant. And since royal dreams are sent by the high gods themselves, we cannot risk misinterpretation. I think that, once you begin, you will find the terror and disgust ebbing. And when we have unraveled this message from the gods, you will be able to take the bold, decisive action that has become the hallmark of your reign."

"You're an eloquent little viper, aren't you?"

And he told me his dream exactly as I had planted it in his lardy skull.

I listened intently as he told me what I knew. I watched his face growing yellower. I was fascinated by the way the sweat was channeled in the creases between his chins.

 40

"Well," he growled, "stop staring at me like an idiot and answer me."

I said, "This dream is undoubtedly a message from the gods and is one of warning."

"That much I know. What am I being warned about?"

"The young prisoner, of course. It is the will of the gods that his life be spared. You are not to put him in a cage, nor cut his head off, nor harm him in any way."

"What do these gods of yours suggest that I do—put my crown on his head with my own hands, then make him really comfortable by slitting my own throat?"

"They would have you contrive his death in a way that will show you as a savior rather than a tyrant."

"How is that possible?"

"You dreamed of drought, did you not? You saw the sky burning, rivers dry, crops scorched, cattle dying."

"Yes."

"That drought is coming. It will strike all the lands of the Middle Sea; they will lie helpless under its burning whip. Only one king in this part of the world shall be given the power to make rain and turn the parched fields green again. That king will be you, if you obey the gods. You have heard of the Golden Fleece?"

"That relic the priests are always yapping about?"

"You speak of it slightingly, sire, but it was the King of Heaven's own garment and enables its wearer to call rain out of a dry sky. It comes from here, from Iolcus, you know. It adorned the statue of thunder-wielding Zeus in the Temple on the Hill—until some three hundred years ago, when it was stolen by a raiding party from Colchis, where it has been kept ever since."

"And we haven't lacked rain in all those three hundred years."

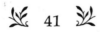

"The weather is about to change, Your Majesty. God-time is not our time; things ripen slowly in the heavens. Now the High Ones decree drought but have promised the power of the Ram to whoever wears its pelt, and that is the power to make rain."

"You speak as if all this were something new. But for six generations now, one crew after another of ne'er-do-wells and criminals on the run have been tapping the treasuries of gullible kings—fitting out ships and sailing away to retake the Fleece. And none of them ever did. They got themselves killed in various ways, or turned pirate or something, but the famous Fleece stayed where it was."

"Yes, sire. And what you are being promised is that Jason also will perish on this quest."

"I can arrange for him to perish right here today and spare myself the expense of ship and crew."

"You ignore the meaning of your dream, O King. The gods want you to send Jason for the Fleece. They promise he will not return, but the Fleece will. And you shall wear it and end the drought—and be so idolized by your people that you will be able to mistreat them to your heart's content and arouse no whisper of complaint."

"I'll give in on one point," he said. "I won't put him in a cage. His presumptuous head shall be quietly separated from his shoulders and flung on the dung heap. That will end the legend of the lost prince."

I spoke silently to my father. "Oh, Hermes, the king is stubborn. Send him a sign, I pray."

I heard the king clapping for a page boy. The lad came running. "Fetch wine," said the king. Then he turned to me. "All this theology makes me thirsty."

The page appeared with two crystal flagons of wine. The king seized his goblet and raised it to his mouth. I was amazed to see the wine shrink away from his lips. He stared into his goblet in disbelief.

"Did you see that?" he muttered. "How's yours, still full?"

I sipped a bit. "Seems all right," I said.

"Give it to me!"

I handed him the great crystal cup. He lifted it to his mouth. Again the wine shrank from his lips. He dashed the cup to the ground; it shattered on the slate path.

"I thirst . . . I thirst! Bring water!" he roared.

The page came running. He bore a pitcher full of water. The king snatched it from him but stopped and poured a little out first to see if it was really there. It splashed on the path. He lifted the pitcher and gulped . . . raised it higher and higher as his mouth sucked frantically. He flung the pitcher from him.

"Misery!" he moaned. "I must drink. I'm dying."

"Ah, King," I said. "The gods have sent you a sign. This is a hint of what drought will be like—when even kings thirst."

"Demon-craft! These are not gods but devils! You are a demon, serving demons! I'll have you burned! Impaled!"

I listened to him, unafraid. He wasn't used to suffering, this fat king, and I knew he was too maddened by thirst to be able to croak out any orders for my execution. I spoke gently. "The gods are being merciful, sire. With this little flick of their whip they are urging you back to the path of righteousness and preserving you from the greater torments of drought."

"All right . . . all right. I'll spare him. I'll send him for that damned Fleece. Do you swear he'll die on the voyage?"

"The Fleece shall return; he shall not. Look, King, your pitcher overflows."

Indeed, the pitcher had righted itself on the path, and water was welling out of it. I picked it up and gave it to him. Very hesitantly, he bent his head to it, touched his mouth to the rim, and sipped. His face sagged with relief as he finally drank.

"Behold, O King, the reward of obedience."

"Here's my ring," he said, "my seal. With it you can speak in my name. Have Jason released and bid him prepare for his voyage. Draw upon the treasury for the necessary expenses. But be prudent, I urge you, be prudent."

E L E V E N

EKION

I FOUND JASON PROWLING the wild beach that lies along the northeast shore and is the first to get the wind. It was a deserted beach, a good place to hide someone.

We walked along the water's edge, and I told him what had happened at court: how I had sowed the king's sleep with visions of drought, of his wrath and his threats, and how Hermes had parched him into submission. "That's why he agreed to let us sail for Colchis," I said. "But he'll change his mind when he regains his courage. So we'd best make haste."

"I'm ready now. When do we start?"

"We must first provide ourselves with ship and crew."

"A ship? Do we build it, or buy it, or simply help ourselves to a vessel of the royal fleet?"

"Hermes will instruct us."

"Does he realize the need for haste? You're always telling me god-time is not our time."

"I shall consult him tonight."

We had paused. He was gazing out to sea. He turned and stared at me. "Do you consider yourself kind-hearted?" he said.

"Never occurred to me."

"I heal by touch. What passes through my hands is some sort of energy—nothing to do with kindness or pity."

"To heal something is a kindness, no matter what you feel."

"Perhaps . . . and perhaps I am meant to be a killer. Obviously my skill at archery was not given me so that I could shoot at trees."

"You'll be finding other things to shoot at. Things that shoot back."

"Consider this," he said. "I'm fond of birds, you know. But I am also fascinated by that butcher among birds, the falcon, the female hawk, larger and stronger than the male. She drops out of the sky upon the pigeon, the lark, the gull . . . drives her hooks into him, stabs him with her beak, and eats the flesh. And I, who have esteemed her victim, also admire the hawk."

"You make too much of it. Falconry has always been the sport of kings. No reason you shouldn't enjoy it without guilt."

"You came to Cythera to trouble my sleep and plant visions. But I dream without your assistance now. She visits me every night."

"Who?"

"A winged girl. She is sleek and powerful and has brass claws on hands and feet. And her eyes—the iris is utterly black and the pupil yellow; they are full of yellow light and cold as moon fire. They freeze my marrow. In the plan of this dream, it seems that I have trained her, for she brings me her prey uneaten. A goat, a lamb, and once—a child."

"I don't like the sound of this. It may be a harpy you've attracted."

"Are there really such things?"

"One of my father's duties is to conduct the newly dead to Tartarus. And he has told me about the Land Beyond Death. Many kinds of demons attend Hades, and the most feared are those hell hags called harpies. They have brass wings and brass claws and carry coiled whips at their girdles. They are used to recapture runaway shades. Indeed, Hades casts them like falcons, and they return to him with their prey."

"Mine has brass claws, but her wings are white leather, delicate as membrane. And she's young. Our age, you know. Not a hag."

"Well, dreams are of unequal value. Not all of them are sent by the gods. Perhaps this creature is simply the feverish vapor of your own fancy."

"No, she's real. She exists outside my mind. Somewhere she stands near a source of light so strong that her shadow is cast across the sea, past the frontiers of mortal sense, into my sleep."

"You know that she dwells beyond the sea?"

"Yes."

"Perhaps she visits you to encourage the quest. Perhaps you will meet her upon your voyage."

T W E L V E

✤ E K I O N

THE KING SUMMONED ME and asked for a report.

"I'm keeping Jason out of public view," I said. "He is making no move to form a party or to claim the throne."

"All right, as far as it goes. But remember, your chief responsibility is to ensure that the lost prince gets himself permanently lost. He is to recapture the Fleece, if possible, but it is to return without him. Is that clear?"

"Yes, Your Majesty."

"To facilitate this worthy aim," he said, "I have arranged to provide you with a ship's company of cutthroats, every man of them briefed on whose throat to cut."

"We'll also need some people to work the ship."

"That part's up to you."

The staff twitched in my hand. The snake lifted its carved head to whisper dryly. It was a message from my father.

Hermes and I walked along the tide line under a moon so bright it branded our shadows on the white sand. There was a heavy surf.

Greenish flames flickered on the mane of the breaking waves. A hot night, but his words were chilling.

"No quest for the Fleece has ever succeeded. All these past voyages, made in sound ships with sufficient crew, have met with disaster."

"Are you recommending an unsound ship and an insufficient crew?"

"You jest, my son, but you speak more wisdom than you know. You don't need a large crew. Three or four good hands can sail a small ship."

"Perhaps, when the winds are favorable. But how about when they blow against us or don't blow at all? Then the ship must be rowed—which takes at least fifty oars."

"You shall sail the way the wind blows. Sooner or later you'll get to Colchis. But with a small loyal band, deserving each other's faith, tested in each other's eyes, a band of brothers."

"The king has slightly different ideas," I said. "He is recruiting a ship's company of trained assassins—who are promised a rich wage, a richer bonus, and a lifetime pension if Jason should meet with some fatal accident along the way. So what am I to do?"

"What I tell you, of course."

"How do I keep my head on my shoulders?"

"Keep a brave heart, and I'll take care of your head."

"Be specific. How do I avoid hiring these murderous characters?"

"Diplomatically, of course. You'll tell them they're hired, give them a sailing date, and make sure to slip anchor before then. By the time you return, they'll all be dead, probably."

"Slip anchor in what?"

"You shall have a ship by then. A shipwright named Argos shall come to you. Do not be deceived by his appearance; he's a master.

Provide him with whatever he requires, and conceal his labors from Pelius."

"Yes, sire. And my crew? That band of brothers?"

"You shall start with your own brothers. They're on the way."

"My own brothers!"

"Autolycus and Daphnis. You haven't forgotten them, have you?"

"Autolycus, yes, he'd be valuable on any adventure. Except . . . "

"Except what?"

"He'll be spending all his time taking care of Daphnis—who can't pass an ordinary day without mishap, let alone the kind of days we'll be passing."

"Daphnis will surprise you."

"He's no longer a nitwit?"

"Sweetest singer since Orpheus. And, unlike that doom-wailer, his nature is as sunny as his voice. His song works enchantment more potent than sword or arrow. You'll be glad to have him along."

T H I R T E E N

❧ E K I O N

WHEN MY BROTHERS JOINED US, we moved camp to a heavily wooded peninsula where the trees ran down to the beach.

Daphnis adored Jason on sight. If Autolycus was jealous, he didn't show it. As for Jason, he received my brothers with more warmth than he had ever shown me. The three of them frisked about, caressing and cuffing each other like half-grown panther cubs, but I stood outside their joyous circle. So, of course, I envied everyone.

In choosing the peninsula for our base camp, I had also selected the best site for shipbuilding. Oak and pine and cedar grew near the sea and would provide our lumber. The ship could be built on the beach and launched right there.

Argos came to us. He didn't look like a master shipwright. He looked like someone a witch had begun to transform into a seal but had left half-done. He was short and smoothly tubby, with very short arms and large hands. He was clad only in a black leather apron, which clung as closely as another skin. Hair and beard were dark brown and very dense. He looked astonishingly like a seal, in fact;

but unlike any beast's, his black eyes smoldered with a furious impatience. He was incapable of understanding why everyone did not share his image of a perfect ship or how anyone could think of anything else. He started to rave as soon as he came.

"You shall use no ax," he told me. "Any touch of metal will blight the soul of the dryad that must invest the timbers and keep them alive."

"Living timbers?"

"If an ordinary deadwood vessel is what you want, you don't employ an Argos. Any ship I build lives upon the water. She sniffs out the best wind and runs before it. She senses the presence of reefs and avoids them. She threads her way among rocks, and beaches where there is no harbor."

"With a ship of yours, one scarcely needs a crew."

"My ship must be served, sir. Must be kept clean and sweet—unblemished in sail and mast, tackle, gear. She must never be left untended because someone will surely steal her."

"First we have to get her built. And it may be difficult to fell trees without using an ax."

The others were lounging about the grove. Jason held a kestrel perched on his leather wristband and was whispering to it. Daphnis sat propped against a fallen log, touching his lyre, not playing a tune but imitating the way the wind sighed among the boughs. Autolycus was catching wasps on the wing and letting them go. None of them seemed to be listening to our conversation, but Autolycus growled, "Daphnis can." I didn't realize he was speaking to me. He prowled closer and said, "Daphnis can do it."

"Do what?"

"Uproot trees." He said to Daphnis, "Do it."

Daphnis arose slowly, holding his lyre in the crook of his left arm. The sun had just sunk, leaving a clear greenish dusk and a wound of light in the west. Standing, waiting, the fragile boy imposed a hush upon us. The birds fell silent. The wind ceased among the boughs. A piece of moon tangled itself in the branches of a cedar. Daphnis raised his right hand; it floated toward the lyre, bringing a single note. He sang of the Beginning:

"A startled light arose from the rubble of Chaos and became the Goddess Eurynome. . . . She danced across the edge of nothingness and the paths of her dancing became the margins of sea and sky. . . . The North Wind pursued her as she fled, dancing. The West Wind and the South Wind and the East Wind joined the chase; they surrounded her. . . . And became the Universal Serpent, Ophion."

I heard a faint sob. Jason was weeping, trying to make no sound. Autolycus was iron-faced, but the iron was wet. The blackness of Argos' hair and beard and apron had made him vanish, all but his glimmering hands. Our circle had enlarged. Deer stood among us, and a pair of gray wolves, ears cocked toward the singer, ignoring the deer. A slouching shadow grew into a bear, shoulders bulking. The moon shook itself free of the cedar, and the animals' eyes became pits of fire.

Man and beast stood rapt as Daphnis sang:

"Eurynome was captive to the winds, and they closed about her. She turned herself into a white bird and flew away. . . . She nested in the sky and laid a clutch of silver eggs, which were the sun and the earth and the planets and all the stars that stud the sky. Upon the earth were trees, flowers, birds, beasts, and man. . . . "

A wrenching, pulling sound began. My brother's voice floated above it and kept us noosed in golden cords even as we watched the trees heaving. Oak and pine and tall cedar, they swayed and jerked in a kind of gigantic dance. One by one they pulled themselves out of the earth and hobbled toward us on their roots and stood among us listening to my brother sing:

"... trees, flowers, birds, beasts, and man. Oh, my brothers, Eurynome means 'far-wandering,' the first name given the moon. . . . Ophion means 'moon-serpent.' And long before there were any gods, there was the All-Mother. The Moon Goddess."

After the song, the deer slid back into the forest, and the wolves vanished. The bear grunted and slouched away. The trees did not return to their holes but hobbled to the beach on their roots and lay down as if to sleep.

F O U R T E E N

E K I O N

WE NOW HAD OUR SHIPWRIGHT and timber to meet his crazed specifications. But we had no tools. Argos carried none; he expected them to appear. He never brought anything anywhere but his talent.

I put Autolycus in charge of procurement.

He left camp that evening and returned at dawn driving an oxcart loaded with axes, mallets, picks, and shovels.

"Brother," I said, "I hope you're not robbing poor farmers."

"Not even rich ones. I'm buying these things."

"What are you using for money?"

"Money."

"And how do you come by it?"

"Same way the king does, from taxes. I happened to meet a tax collector on the road and persuaded him to let me carry his bag of gold."

"Persuaded?"

"A little knock on the head," Autolycus said. "He found it persuasive."

"You robbed a royal tax collector—"

"Who had been robbing farmers. Actually, what I did, you might say, is give them back their money. The king is taxing them too heavily; it's bad policy."

"Knowing Pelius as I do, brother, I am certain he would not appreciate your method of reform."

"Well, the king did agree to finance this voyage, didn't he?"

"Yes, but he hates to keep such promises."

So Autolycus slipped away every dusk and reappeared every dawn. We would be awakened by the clanking of tools and would arise to see the great sun lifting itself out of the sea and ox and boy and wagon crawling blackly across the redness.

Upon this dawn we heard the clanking, but everything else was different. The wagon floated strangely in the air; when it came closer, we saw that it was being borne like a litter by two giant figures. Upon it sprawled the limp shape of Autolycus.

It was always a wonder to me how swiftly Jason could move without seeming to. He was streaking now across the grass. He was confronting two huge men. They stood listening to him, then gently lowered the wagon to the ground. One of them stooped and lifted Autolycus as if he were a baby, then laid him at Jason's feet. Jason was kneeling, touching my brother's head.

Daphnis was there, too, now. I heard him whimper. Without looking at him, Jason raised his hand and the whimpering ceased. Argos had arisen by now and stood there confused, glaring at everyone. I strolled across the clearing to where the strangers stood. I had to find out if they had been sent by Pelius, and, if so, to send them away again. I was getting quite good at this. They were magnificent specimens. Standing there in the pink new sunlight, they were carved of rosy marble. Twins obviously, but not identical. One was slightly bigger.

Autolycus was sitting up now, leaning against Jason, who was holding a cup to his mouth, as Daphnis hovered near.

"Greetings," I said. "I am Ekion, son of Hermes, and herald to King Pelius. And my brother is the one you brought out of the forest. He is still in no condition to thank you, so I do it in his stead."

The larger one spoke. "My name is Castor. And this is my brother, Pollux. We are princes of Sparta, sons of Leda, who is wife to King Tyndareus."

I had to think quickly. They called themselves sons of Leda, but not of her husband. Adding that fact to their gigantic stature and their beauty, I deduced that their mother had told them she had entertained some god who had become their father. I wanted to acknowledge this, but to leave myself some opening in case I was misreading things. Luckily, I was trained in tact.

"Fair sirs," I said, "had you not told me your parentage, I should have guessed you for the sons of a god. Zeus, most likely. Or Apollo, perhaps. Or Ares."

"You are courteous," said the smaller one. "Zeus it was who honored our mother, putting on the shape of a swan for the purpose."

"I welcome you, sons of Zeus. And so shall my brothers, when Autolycus is on his feet again and Daphnis has ceased fretting. We are your cousins, of course. Jason also, he there who is mending my brother's head. But tell me what happened."

"We were on our way here," said Castor, "following the road where it runs between sea and forest, when we saw an oxcart coming. But we saw a bear spring out of the woods, and kill the ox with one blow of its paw. And were amazed to see the driver attack the bear with a knife. The beast caught him only a glancing blow, luckily, but it was enough to send him flying. The bear went after him, and I went after the bear."

"You killed the bear by yourself?"

"It was in a rage, and I had to kill it. I was sorry to. I like bears. Often wrestle with them back home, for I have run out of men to contend with."

"And what do you do for sport?" I said to the smaller one, who had eyes like chips of blue ice.

"It is more difficult for me," Pollux said. "I am a boxer rather than a wrestler. And bears don't box."

"He has also run out of men to fight," said Castor. "And for him there is no such thing as a friendly bout. Whom he hits he kills."

"No, neither of us can find anyone to fight," said Pollux. "That's why we have come here. We have heard that you are about to go after the Golden Fleece, a journey that offers an array of monsters and other worthy antagonists."

And that is how the Twins enrolled themselves in the crew of the *Argo*. And we were glad to have them. Handling the tree trunks and the huge rocks, they seemed as strong as Titans—and there were two of them.

F I F T E E N

E K I O N

ANOTHER STRANGER CAME into the clearing, of medium height and thin as sword blade, black-haired, black-browed, and of mushroom complexion. "Looks like trouble," I thought. "Must be one of the king's cutthroats."

Suddenly he smiled at me, and I was amazed. I had never seen a smile like that, a glittering ghastly spasm, indescribably ferocious. Curiosity pulled me across the grass toward him, and I couldn't help peering into his mouth. He opened it wide.

They weren't teeth. He had none. Instead, he wore two brass blades curved to the shape of his gums; they were what gave him his dazzling death's-head grin.

His jaws snapped shut. He grinned again. It took all my self-control not to shudder. He spoke in a hoarse voice, hardly more than a whisper.

"Are you Jason, prince of Iolcus?"

"No, sir. I am his cousin, Ekion, herald to the king."

"I have come to see Jason."

"May I know your business?"

"I wish to join his crew and journey after the Fleece."

"Was it the king who sent you?"

"No one sent me. I am not to be sent. I go where fancy takes me."

I didn't believe him. He looked too much like an assassin not to be one. The more I studied him, the uneasier I grew. He was in his mid-twenties, perhaps, but I saw now the cause of his pallor. His face was a web of faint scars. And when I dropped my eyes, I saw that his left hand was missing. A polished metal spike was attached to his wrist; it seemed to grow right out of the stump.

"You are staring at me," he whispered.

"I'm sorry."

"It's all right, lad; it's understandable. I'm not a boastful man, you know, but I wear my badges of honor in plain sight. I have no choice."

"Battle wounds?"

"Ex-wounds. Scars and replacement parts. My teeth were knocked out one by one, but I waited until they were all gone before I got these beauties. Oh, they are beautiful if fighting is your business. See here."

He scooped up a handful of pebbles and put them in his mouth, working his jaws. I could hear the brass blades grinding the pebbles. He spat dust, and said, "There are times when you're so hemmed in you can't use weapons—only kick and punch and bite. Think how useful these are then . . . how much better than ordinary teeth. And as for this item"—he held up his spike—"very useful, too. Where I'm concerned, there is no such thing as unarmed combat."

"I can appreciate that, sir."

"My problem is I always have to be first in a fight. When I hear war cries and the clash of arms, a fire burns in my gut that can only be cooled by blood. Unfortunately, the blood is usually my own. I'm always charging in too soon and getting sliced up before I can do enough. It's my one fault as a warrior. Injuries make me miss almost as much action as if I were a coward."

I couldn't decide whether he had been sent by Pelius or not. "You put me in an awkward position," I said. "I'm under orders from the king. It is I who am responsible for enrolling the crew. And the king has forbidden me to take anyone without his recommendation. But you say you do not know him?"

"That is correct."

"I'm more than eager to enlist a man of your valor and special attributes. Anyone would want you for a shipmate. But what can I do?"

He stepped closer and smiled. His brass toothwork glittered like the hinges of hell.

"You're lying," he said softly. "I'm going to bite off your nose."

I tried to spring away, but his spike had slid behind the waistband of my tunic and I could not move.

"Don't bite me! Don't bite me!" I cried. "I'm not lying!"

"Of course you are. My young friends Castor and Pollux sent me word they had joined your crew, and they do not come from your foolish king."

"The Twins—will they vouch for you?"

"Certainly."

"You're hired, then. Let me go. And please stop looking at my nose that way. You see, I had to make sure you were *not* sent by the king."

"What do you mean?"

"He wants to supply us with a crew of assassins, all pledged to murder Jason. That's why I have to be careful. Believe me, sir, I want you on my side in any fighting that is to be done."

"I thought heralds never fought. Aren't you exempt from harm by both sides?"

"In ordinary warfare, yes. But the monsters that beset our route tend to eat you first and examine your credentials later."

"I've come to the right place. My name is Idas, prince of Messene."

"Welcome aboard."

S I X T E E N

E K I O N

ARGOS DECIDED HE NEEDED some metalwork done. He wouldn't touch it himself; he worked only in wood. "It is well we are in a land where expert smiths abound," he told me. "You shall choose one of them to do what we need."

"Impossible," I said.

"A concept I do not acknowledge," he said.

"The smiths here serve Hephaestus and are considered priests. The chief smith is a court dignitary. If I bring this work to any forge in the land, the king will hear about it immediately. He will understand that we are secretly building a vessel and recruiting our own crew—and the consequences thereof will be exceedingly painful, not to say fatal."

"All this is none of my concern," said Argos. "My task is to get the ship built, yours is to get me whatever I need. The metalwork must be done by an expert—but not necessarily at his own smithy. We'll dig a fire pit right here. He can do his work right on the spot."

"Bring someone here to spy out our whole operation? Brilliant!"

"Stop this negative nonsense and fetch me a smith."

"We cannot and will not use anyone outside our own company."

"I don't care how you get him or what you do with him afterward. Have those Spartan bullies kidnap him, if you like. When the work is done, you can throw him in the fire. Then he can't tattle."

I saw there was no reasoning with this madman and walked away. Then I had an idea. I journeyed half a day to the great smithy, which was in a cave in a hill near the palace. I entered that huge, smoky, clanking place and found my friend Rufus at an anvil, hammering on a red-hot bar of iron. He looked like a young fire demon in the flickering shadows. His red hair seemed to shoot sparks.

I was very glad to see him. He appeared to have grown since we had last met—seemed to have widened; his arms and legs were ridged with muscle. He was bare-armed in a leather apron. His left hand held the tongs that clamped the bar; his right hand held a mallet.

He dropped the sledge, took the tongs in both hands, and lifted the red-hot bar off the anvil. He dropped it into a bucket of water, and steam hissed out. He still hadn't seen me standing there. He poured the steaming water into a trough, poured in cold water from another bucket, and left the bar to cool.

He raised his head. His smile flashed. My heart danced. He liked me! Suddenly, to my enormous surprise, he embraced me. I was unused to this. The clanging of many hammers became a music of rejoicing. I smelled burning charcoal, leather, steam, hot iron, sweat. My cold heart warmed enough to take in the strange idea of friendship. This made me shy. I pushed him away.

"I must talk to you," I said. "It's important."

"Wait for me at the foot of the hill."

This day gulls had flown inland. Their screeching sounded pure as song after the clanging of metal in the cave. And the fresh golden air was intoxicating. I saw Rufus bounding downhill like a goat.

We walked toward the woods. "Well, tell," he said. "I haven't heard anything important for a long time."

"Wait till we get into the woods."

"Is it very secret?"

"Dead secret."

"Well, tell me something. Tell more lies about your relatives on Olympus."

"Some of them are down here," I said. "I just met two cousins. The Dioscuri."

"Who?"

"The twin sons of Zeus. Also princes of Sparta."

I described Castor and Pollux, and how they had saved Autolycus from the bear. Then I realized he didn't know who Autolycus was, or Daphnis, and I told about them, too, and about Jason. Then about Argos and Idas. And before we had reached the great oak, I had told him all about what we were doing and why. I had not meant to tell so much. But, seeing the wonder on his face, I couldn't help myself.

Then I realized I had done the right thing. He turned away from me and spoke in a strangled voice. "I'd like to join your company," he said.

"A novice in the high service of the smith-god. Are you permitted to resign?"

"Of course not. I'll simply vanish."

"They'll be after you hammer and tongs."

"Why should they find me? I'll be on that wild east shore with you. Then we'll be out to sea. And we shall either die gloriously or return as heroes."

I wanted to say yes. Argos would have someone to work his metal, and I would have a friend of my own for the voyage. But I was afraid to consent. A runaway novice would infuriate the entire guild and start a great manhunt. It was a terrible risk. What I had hoped was that he would be able to do our work secretly at his own forge.

"I can make myself useful," he said. "You must have a lot of iron-work to do: the beak for your ship, swords, daggers, spearheads, armor. I also work in copper and brass. And if you have gold and rubies and such, I'll whip up some baubles to win the hearts of maidens at every landfall. In fact, I'll bring gold and diamonds with me. They keep them in a vault, but I can cast keys, too."

"My brother the thief will have much employment for you."

"Then I may join?"

"Yes."

S E V E N T E E N

❦ E K I O N

THE SHIP STOOD COMPLETE except for painting and tarring. It was a marvel—slender, swift, and with two brilliant new features: a pivoted rudder board instead of the great clumsy stern oar and a mast that tilted the sail for a quartering wind, permitting us to outrace and outmaneuver any other vessel on the sea. Or so our shipwright claimed.

He had also made a skiff to be carried on deck, using materials never before used: whalebone for ribs and struts; not planks for its hull but whale hide, scraped membrane-thin and tough as oiled silk. In making the oars, he had allowed for the enormous strength of the Twins. He used polished ash stiffened with rhinoceros horn. Under great stress, they bent like bows but did not break; when bent, they snapped back, adding to the titanic power of the Twins' stroke.

"It's a pirate skiff, really," Argos told us. "Fleeing or pursuing, it will outrun anything. I learned its design when I voyaged to the Land Beyond the Dawn, where dwell little men with tilted eyes and parasols growing out of their heads. They carry curved knives and live on fish heads and tangerines. This is their design, but they never made a skiff to match mine, and their oars are flimsy things."

Finally the ship was caulked and painted. There was never any question about her name. Rufus melted gold and mixed it with pine-nut oil and painted *Argo* in letters of gold across her stern. *Argo* was her name, and we who sailed her became known as the Argonauts.

EIGHTEEN

🌿 E K I O N

THREE DAYS OUT OF PORT, we were cutting through the water under bright skies. I was at the bow watching points of light dance on the ruffled sea. We were all on deck. Rufus and Idas stood at the weather rail, deep in their endless discussion of new fittings for the Messenean's wrist stump. My redheaded friend was spending entirely too much time on that lopped lout. I was jealous.

Daphnis sat on the iron block that was Rufus's deck anvil. He was touching his lyre. By the goofy rapt look on his face I knew he was composing a verse. Autolycus was curled at the foot of the anvil, asleep—but with a pantherine grace; he seemed poised for leaping even as he slept.

The Twins were sparring. Idas had told them how dueling was done in his savage land. Enemies tied their left arms together and fought with knives. Castor and Pollux stood on the deck, left arm bound to left arm with a length of anchor chain, striking at each other with imaginary daggers. A point would be scored when one would slice past the other's guard and touch his body with the edge

of his fist. They were hitting as lightly as they could, but with enough force to cave in the ribs of anyone else.

Jason had climbed the mast and was perched on top, his legs wound around the spar. He was swaying in the wind. It was slackening now; he was waiting for it to blow gently enough for him to dive off the mast and be able to overtake the ship without our having to circle back.

Daphnis came to me and said, "I'm doing a sea song, using the cry of the wind, the creak of blocks, the rattle of tackle, the lisp of waters, all that we hear. At sea we tune ourselves to these sounds and are startled when one of them stops or a new sound comes."

He spoke softly; his sweet murmuring and the occasional plink of the lyre had begun to put me to sleep on my feet. And in that sun-dazed half-sleep I seemed to be entering an old dream again, to be standing at the stump-water ocean watching a tiny visionary ship sail into disaster. I heard again an odd gurgling, rushing sound. My eyes snapped open, and I saw that, sure enough, we were sailing toward two huge boulders that had suddenly appeared. They stood about a quarter of a mile apart. But I remembered what had happened in my vision, and I shouted to Argos to put about. But found that I was shouting into a violent gust.

The wind carried away my voice. We drove straight forward to the passage between the rocks. And I saw to my horror that the dream was coming true: the rocks were beginning to hurtle toward each other over the face of the water.

If my dream had been truly prophetic, then the rocks were driven by an evil intelligence and were intending to catch us between them. I remembered what I had seen: the hull cracking like a walnut, the men crushed, the bloody water. The wind was blowing harder and harder; the sail was taut. Sheets of spray curled at our bow, rising in a beautiful double arc and falling into a wake behind us.

I saw that we were going fast enough to pass between the rocks before they could meet. But even as I thought this, the rocks picked up speed and bowled terrifically over the water, coming straight at us, one on each side.

They were huge, towering high above the mast. They were massive chunks of mountain risen from the bottom of the sea to destroy us. They were very close now. I could see the mosses that grew upon them, purple and green, and their crust of barnacles.

Argos put over the helm. The ship answered, swinging away from the rocks, and we were darting off, as the rocks hurtled toward each other. Oh, how I hoped they would collide, shattering themselves.

But then—sickening sight—they swerved simultaneously and began to pursue us, plowing through the water, side by side. We had gained by our turn; they were farther behind. And the wind was still blowing hard, driving us on. But as I watched, the rocks grew larger and larger.

They were directly astern. I couldn't see whether they were sliding along the surface of the water or forging through it. Both seemed impossible. Yet these boulders were coming at us with terrific speed. Our only hope was for the wind to blow harder.

I prayer for it to blow harder. And my prayer was answered. The wind picked up. It howled through the rigging. Jason still rode atop the mast; he couldn't have climbed down if he had wanted to. He had to cling with arms and legs, or he would have been blown off like a leaf.

It was blowing a half-gale now. Our sail cupped the wind and the *Argo* flew over the water. I saw the rocks dwindle behind us. And I thanked whatever god had heard my prayer. Too soon. No sooner had I thanked him than the wind dropped. It was amazing. One moment it was blowing a half-gale, the next moment hardly a whisper of wind. The sail flapped. We wallowed. And the rocks rushed upon us.

I heard a shout. Whiteness fell from the sky like a swan plunging. It was Jason diving in a long arc from the top of the mast, arms and legs taut, hair sculptured in the speed of his fall. He entered the water cleanly and surfaced well beyond the ship, heading for the rocks.

He swam so fast he seemed to be skimming over the bright skin of the water. I saw that he wanted to meet the rocks as far from the ship as possible. But why? What could he do when he met them? He would affect them no more than a bird sharpening its beak.

I saw the rocks flinging spray as they braked in the water. They were stopping! I saw them drift sideways, away from each other, as if parting to leave a safe passage for the swimmer. Less and less did I understand what I was seeing.

Jason swam straight on, brown arms flashing. Something white floated behind him. It was his tunic. Then I saw why the rocks had drifted apart, and realized that they were indeed directed by a living intelligence. For they were changing direction. They were again rushing toward each other. They had separated only to give themselves space to pick up speed, intending to catch Jason between them. They were closing like giant jaws; they wouldn't even leave a corpse if they met upon him. He would be a pinkish spot spreading on the waters.

Gulls seemed to know they were being offered a meal. They dived, screaming, plunging so close they risked being caught between the rocks, which were almost touching now. The diving gulls obscured the swimmer. The huge boulders struck each other with a horrid grinding crash.

I couldn't see Jason. I saw only gulls and flying spray and rock

dust. Suddenly the gulls vanished. More slowly, the dust cleared. The boulders had disappeared. Had they shattered themselves upon each other? Or dissolved again into vision? No—they had been there. Fragments of rock littered the water. I was holding my breath. I didn't even know I had stopped breathing until I heard the tortured air moaning as it forced itself out.

What was I hoping? Did I want to see the black head breaking water beyond the litter? Or did I want to detect blood on the water? I seemed to feel my eyes burn, hungry as a gull's for a glimpse of redness among the rock litter, or a bone, or a gobbet of flesh.

Whatever I hoped, I saw him surface, not merely showing head and shoulders, but broaching like a porpoise, rising straight out of the sea until his feet were clear, shedding diamonds of waterdrops, then turning in the air and arching back, shouting exultantly . . . uttering a victory yell that was impossibly loud coming from that slender frame. His voice bowled across the still air like thunder, rattling our oxhide stays.

We were all laughing and shouting, embracing one another and dancing on deck as he swam slowly now toward us, pushing through rock fragments as he came. But one stone about the size of a fist followed him as he swam. And when he reached the stern and was scrambling up to us, that white stone leaped out of the sea and landed on deck. It rolled to his feet.

It was as if this single stone were the survivor of those boulders that had dashed themselves to death upon each other—as if it had inherited their weird energy and menacing intelligence and now offered itself to the victor.

NINETEEN

E K I O N

FOOD AND WATER WERE RUNNING LOW; we decided to stop at the first island we sighted. But the wind fell off, and for the next two days we crawled across a landless sea. On the morning of the third day the wind freshened, and by midday we had sighted a small, hilly island.

"It's called Bebrycos," said Argos. "But I don't think we should put in. It has a bad reputation."

"You've said that about every other island we've passed," said Jason. "What's wrong with this one?"

"I don't remember exactly," said Argos. "Something about a king who doesn't like visitors—or maybe likes them too well and never lets them go. We'd better pass it by."

"And when we come to the next island, you'll remember something bad about that one," said Jason. "In the meantime, we'll run out of food and water. We're landing here."

"You'll take the skiff, then," said Argos. "I'll stand offshore."

I saw Jason's jaw muscles throb and his gray eyes darken. But all he said was, "Find a bottom and drop anchor. We'll take the skiff."

Actually, we knew this was safer, although we were all getting irritated at the way Argos would rather risk our lives than endanger a plank of his precious ship. Still, we knew that most islanders did not welcome strangers, and that it was better to sneak ashore than sail boldly into an unknown harbor.

We spent the rest of the afternoon hunting a good place to anchor—which was hard to find because the bottom shelved sharply here and the water stayed deep almost all the way to the beach. We didn't dare anchor so close to shore. A war canoe could dart out swiftly as a dragonfly and put a party aboard us before we could get under way.

We sailed all around the island without finding a place. Then Jason had an idea. By this time his rock had grown to boulder size and rolled behind him wherever he went, sliding off the deck and surging after him when he swam. Jason instructed Rufus to make a harness for the rock.

The smith went to his deck anvil and wrought rods and chains into a strong openwork iron nest and attached it to a long cable. Jason spoke to the rock; it rolled into its harness, slid to the edge of the deck, then overboard and sank. The cable stretched taut, and the *Argo* swung at a bow mooring where there was no bottom.

We rowed to an empty beach and struck inland. We picked up animal tracks and followed them through a screen of trees to a stream. It was a lovely place, girded by trees and floored by pine needles, and the stream widened into a deep pond. We stripped and dived in, frolicking like children.

I climbed out and went to see what lay beyond the wood. I came to an open space. I was standing in a kind of natural arena, a large grassy meadow cupped by low blue hills. The place was empty, humming with silence. I saw movement up one slope and climbed a path, threading among boulders. On one of them sat a girl weeping.

"Why do you weep, beautiful maiden?"

"Oh, I'd rather be ugly!"

"That's something only a beautiful girl can say."

"I don't care, I do, I do. I wish I was ugly as a toad. Then that innocent boy wouldn't have to die."

"You'd better tell me all about it."

"But you're a stranger."

"Secrets should be told only to strangers."

"You say 'only' a lot, don't you? Who are you?"

"Only a stranger . . . tell me of this love and this death."

"You talk like singing."

"Wait till you meet my brother."

"We have this king here, you see, and he's a terrible man. He knows that someone has asked my hand in marriage, and he means to kill him."

"Are you the king's daughter?"

"No, sir. I'm his wife's sister."

"Why does he wish to kill your suitor? Is the lad so unworthy?"

"He'll kill anyone who wants to marry me. He's saving me for himself."

"But he's married to your sister, you say."

"After he kills her, he'll marry me. Then, when he's tired of me, my younger sister should be old enough."

"The man's a monster."

"Yes, sir. That's what he is. Everyone hates him. But they fear him even more. And he enjoys being feared. And kills anyone who displeases him. Now that poor boy has displeased him, only because he was unlucky enough to fall in love with me. And so he goes into the ring today."

"Ring?"

"Boxing ring, where the king does his killing. He challenges someone to a fight and kills him in the ring."

"Can't anyone stand up to him?"

"Oh no. No one has a chance. You'll see for yourself. He'll be coming here soon to warm up."

She sobbed again, gazing at me sideways through tears that seemed to magnify her green eyes.

"I may be able to help you," I said.

"Help me?"

"To escape this island. I'll go talk to the others."

"I'll come with you."

"No, stay here. If they agree, I'll come back for you. But you must promise not to say one word about your wicked brother-in-law and the way he kills people in the ring. If you do, we'll never get off this island."

"Why not?"

"We have some hotheads who love to fight, no matter what the odds. One in particular considers himself quite a boxer. If he hears about this king, he'll challenge him immediately."

"Oh no! He mustn't! That would be terrible. I won't say a word. Go quickly, sir, and arrange my rescue."

"Too late," I groaned.

Coming toward us, picking their way among the rocks, were Jason and Pollux.

"There you are," called Jason. "We've been looking all over for you. The kegs are full. We're ready to go."

"Who's your friend?" said Pollux softly.

They stood there, their tunics white-hot in the sun. Pollux's hair was a nimbus of golden flame, and Jason's black hair held blue light in the cusp of its wave, like a blackbird's wing.

"This is a young lady of the court," I said. "The queen's sister. She needs rescuing."

Her eyes had never left Pollux's face. She began her tale, but dreamily, almost joyously, as if offering a gift to the young men who had come suddenly and gorgeously out of nowhere—like gods. They listened greedily.

"Do they fight down there?" asked Jason, pointing to the meadow.

"Yes," she said. "The people sit up here when they're invited. Look, here he comes! That's the king! That's Amycus!"

A troop of spearmen were trotting across the field. Following them was an enormous brute of a man who had placed himself between the shafts of an oxcart and was pulling it easily at a half-run. Two oxen trotted alongside. The huge man broke into a gallop as the soldiers divided into two ranks, allowing the oxcart to pass between. The king shouted with laughter and dropped the shafts.

He stood there clad in a leather clout, seeming about eight feet tall and wide as two men. He was hairy as a bear; we couldn't see his muscles under the dense pelt, but knew they were there. He raised his hand. One of the spearmen, the largest, was carrying a club instead of a spear—a huge bludgeon carved out of hardwood. He raised his club and smashed it down on his master's head.

The club broke cleanly in two. The soldier stood staring at the king, holding the handle. We heard the king laugh and saw him clap the man on the shoulder. The man staggered, straightened smartly, and marched back into the ranks. Amycus raised his arm again. An ox was led toward him. He grasped its horns, hunched his furry shoulders in a curious way, and seemed to be looking deeply into the animal's eyes.

Suddenly he struck with his head, butting the ox terrifically between its horns. Now, any horned beast wears a bridge of heavy bone under its hide between the horns that is stronger than the horn itself. The king's head struck full on this armored brow. For a moment I thought he was trying to break his head on the ox in some sacrificial rite. But it was the ox that fell, blood streaming from its nostrils. The soldiers shouted and beat their shields with their spears.

"That's how he finishes them off," murmured the girl. "With his head. If he doesn't kill them with his fists, he butts them to death."

"Oh, glory, glory," I heard Pollux whisper. "This is the match I've been looking for."

"Don't even think about it!" I cried. "You'll kill us all!"

Horrified, I saw the helmets swivel toward us as Pollux's exultant yell sounded in my ears. I tried to grasp his arm, but he tore away from me and was bounding down the hill, yelling all the way. We followed the madman down the hill. I kept telling myself I could not afford to show fear. So I raised my white staff and walked slowly to where Pollux stood confronting the king.

Observing Amycus from the hillside, I had seen how big and powerful he was, but wasn't able to pick out detail. Now, standing close to that head that had hammered down an ox, I couldn't believe it belonged to a human body. It was totally bald, burnished a rich brown, taut and hard as a bullhide shield. The forehead was a corrugated ridge of bone. His face was meager; the features were huddled beneath that mallet of a brow. The nose was flattened, the eyes deeply pocketed, his mouth a thin pucker. His neck, surprisingly, was long but very thick, as wide as his head; it was one length of muscle, giving that murderous whiplike power to his butting.

"Amycus, king of Bebrycos," I intoned loudly and clearly, "I come vested with the sacred office of herald to bear greetings from my lord, Pelius, king of Iolcus, whose herald I am, traveling on embassy extraordinary with this royal expedition to recover the Golden Fleece. The Middle Sea we ply in a ship called the *Argo*, and have put in here to ask your hospitality, also provisions of food and water, promising you the gratitude of Pelius the Impatient, monarch of Iolcus."

"Shut up, runt," grunted the king. "One more word out of you and

I'll shove that staff where it'll do the most good. Your friend here says he wants to fight."

We heralds, whose business is mostly with kings, are trained to ignore anger and seek to extract some profit from rudeness. I kept smiling, and said smoothly, "Yes, sire, that is the rest of what I have to tell you. Our champion, Pollux, son of Zeus, prince of Sparta, and the foremost pugilist on this earth, seeks the honor of engaging you, Amycus, in fisticuffs—and trusts that, according to the usages of such contests, you will extend a royal hospitality to his entire party."

By this time the rest of the crew had joined us: Daphnis, bearing his lyre; Autolycus stalking beside him, wary as a cat; Idas, glaring about at the soldiers, itching, I knew, to fight them one by one. And Castor, who had shouldered up close to the king, stood there with his brother, staring up at the huge, hairy man.

"What are you, twins?" he growled.

"Yes, sir," said Castor. "I am Castor, the wrestler. Do you have a champion for me to fight? A brother, perhaps. Or someone else big enough to make a contest of it? Or perhaps you would prefer to wrestle instead of box?"

"Stop that," said Pollux. "He's mine."

"Easy, lads, easy," said the king. "There's enough of me to go around. I'll fight you one after the other. You have my promise, Castor. After I kill this one, it'll be your turn."

"Thank you," said Castor. "But I'm afraid I'll be missing my turn."

"Ho, ho," rumbled Amycus. "You're fine lads. I'm going to enjoy this. We'll make a real event of it. We'll fight this afternoon. Until then, rest yourselves. Until the match you are my honored guests. And after the match, that is, after I kill both twins, I'll fight the rest of you, either separately or together. All except the two little ones . . ."
He pointed at Daphnis. "You shall be my harp boy, blue eyes. And

you, master herald, you'll be less talkative after I cut out your tongue. Until then, enjoy yourselves."

We went to the stream and rested in the shade of the trees. The Twins had stayed behind to choose the ground for the match. Idas and Autolycus and Rufus were deep in discussion. I knew they were planning something. I could see that Jason wanted to join them, but I held him back for a moment.

"Why are you letting him fight?" I said. "We could make a break for it. They're guarding the skiff, but we could get into the surf, perhaps, and swim to the *Argo*."

"I can't stop Pollux from fighting," he said. "I wouldn't if I could. You must allow a man to do what he does best." He smiled at me. "You did well today. I was impressed by your eloquence. And we shall try to see that so clever a tongue does not fall under the knife."

I watched the slaves dig a great pit to roast crayfish in. The sea here was colder than our home waters and the crayfish the most delicious we had ever tasted. A haunch of venison was turning on a spit; another spit held an entire lamb.

But the king's generosity was wasted. Jason warned us to eat very sparingly. "Don't stuff yourselves," he whispered. "We may have to move fast after the fight."

The spearmen who were guarding us happily ate most of the food, and the slaves devoured the rest. Castor and Pollux were still at the arena.

I was restless. I strolled back to the arena. The hillside was filling with people seating themselves on the boulders along the slopes; from there they could watch the fight comfortably. A vast throng was gathering. I saw the Twins in a corner of the field and went to them.

"Have you chosen your ground?" I said.

"Here," said Castor.

It was a place where the field tapered toward a cliff face of sheer rock, which stretched up about ten feet before sloping.

"Why here?" I said. "Why not in the middle of the field where your speed would give you a chance? He'll simply corner you here and pound you to pieces."

"That's exactly what I want him to think," said Pollux.

"May the gods smile upon you, my brave Pollux. But I still wish you'd fight him out there."

I stayed with them, waiting for the king to come. People were flocking in now, thronging the slopes. Some sat on boulders; others leaned against them or sat on the ground. Some stood. It looked as if the entire population of the island had come to see the fight. Vendors passed among them selling prawns, honeycombs, and melons.

The king came, surrounded by spearmen, trailed by slaves. He wore a blue tunic and a golden crown. I raised my staff to salute him, but he brushed past me and went to Pollux.

"Are you prepared to die?"

"I am prepared to fight."

"Have you chosen your ground?"

"Here's where we stand. This rock wall is one boundary. Then twelve paces out and across."

The king turned to the soldiers. "Pace it off and stand your pickets."

An officer marched off twelve paces from the rock wall, then another twelve paces parallel to the wall—and placed his men a pace apart along the boundaries, making a square with the wall at one end. The armored men formed a hedge of iron.

A trumpeter raised his horn and blew a clear call. He dropped his horn and addressed the vast crowd now blackening the slopes: "People of Bebrycos, you have been summoned here to watch your king, Amycus, Guardian of the Coast and Hammer of Justice, destroy another Middle Sea pirate who dares enter our land without invitation. Watch him perish. After destroying this man, who boasts of being a son of Zeus and prince of Sparta, our king will fight his twin. After that, he will fight the others of the crew, one at a time or all at once, as they choose."

As this was being announced, the king's slaves were stripping their master. He shed tunic and crown and loomed like a furry demon. The sunlight glinted on his naked head, making it glow like a brass helmet. The crier blasted his horn again. The fight began.

Pollux was a big man, but he looked pitifully small as he retreated before the hairy giant. As I had feared, the king owned every advantage in this tightly penned space. He could corner Pollux, maul him with his great fists until he worked in close enough for his death butt. Yet Pollux himself, with Castor advising, had chosen this place. Why? I couldn't figure it out. Nor could I read anything in the faces of the others who were watching the fight.

Castor stood impassive as a block of marble; his yellow mane, ruffled by the wind, was the only thing about him that moved. Idas stood there, metal fangs flashing as he drew his lips back in a mirthless grin. Every once in a while he glanced at the hedge of spearmen, and I knew how avid he was to be at their throats instead of watching others fight.

It was strange what was happening in the ring. It was more like a dance than a fight. Amycus shuffled after Pollux, trying to block him off, but the blond youth simply flowed away from those fists and from those massive furred arms, moving head and torso just enough to escape the flailing blows, stepping away from the bull-like charges. Eyes pale as frozen lakes, yellow crest gleaming, he was untouched, although Amycus had aimed a hundred blows at him. Untouched—and he had not yet struck back at the king.

Jason, I saw, was smiling. Rufus was blazing with excitement—

fire-red, twitching his shoulders, shuffling, eager to fight himself. I realized, with a lost pang, that I was with those who simply did not know what fear was. The thing about cowardice is that you can usually comfort yourself because it is so common. Other people, you think, are just as frightened as you are. But in this group I felt very much alone.

I looked quickly at Daphnis. Surely this frail poet must be terrified. But I'll be cursed if he didn't wear that goofy simper of his, gazing raptly at the fighters.

Pollux had changed tactics now. Where before he had been moving very thriftily, just evading the king's blows, now he began to leap. He sprang backward from one end of the ring to the other. As soon as he touched ground, he leaped to the other side. Amycus rushed after him. He was no longer cool; he was losing his temper. He charged again, more swiftly this time. But just as he reached him, Pollux rose straight into the air. He leaped higher than the king's head, leaned upon air, and launched a scything sidewise kick. Amycus ducked, and the foot whizzed past his head. I thought, "Why does he duck? Kicking that head is kicking a rock; any foot must break."

And Amycus must have thought the same thing at the same time. For Pollux landed with knees bent and immediately sprang into the air again, kicking again at the king's head—and this time the king did not duck. But the foot did not meet the head. It was exquisitely aimed. It swerved in the air, caught the ear of Amycus, and tore it half away. The side of the king's face was painted with blood.

This did not weaken him but seemed to give him new strength. He bellowed with rage and charged again. This time, as Pollux sprang away, he did not rush after him but dove through the air—dove halfway across the ring, catching Pollux with his shoulder and hurling him against the hedge of armored men, who pushed him back

into the ring. The king was all over him now, crowding him, mauling him with his fists. One roundhouse punch caught him between shoulder and elbow; his left arm went limp, as if broken. His mouth bled. The crowd on the slopes began to roar for the kill.

But it was as if the taste of his own blood refreshed the Spartan. He began to move swiftly again, stepping away from Amycus, dancing around him, leaping away, swaying out of reach—as if the wind of the giant's fists were bending him away like a reed.

The king was breathing heavily now, almost panting. And Pollux began to strike back, using only his right arm. He was wise enough not to break his fist on the king's face. He was hitting at the body. The great rib cage sounded like a drum as Pollux beat a lightning tattoo on the king's torso. Nine blows he struck, and was away before Amycus could answer with one. It was hard to tell the effect of these blows. But from the sound of it, the king's body must have been one big bruise.

And now you could see his decision forming: to plow forward no matter what the punishment, take all the Spartan's punches for the sake of using his mallet head. It seemed to be working. Pollux retreated, but straight back, without springing away. Perhaps he was too tired to leap. Amycus came at him, shuffling, crouching like a huge hairy spider moving toward a white moth.

Pollux was back against the wall now. He was slumping against the rock. And Amycus was upon him. He did not punch but grasped the boy's shoulders, drew back that boulder of a head, and speed itself combined with the thick presence of death to slow everything. We saw that fatal head smashing toward the beautiful face of the Spartan twin.

And then the golden head slid away more swiftly than the wink of an eye . . . moved just enough so that the king's head barely grazed him and smashed into the rock wall.

🌿 91 🌿

The crowd had fallen silent. Now it emitted one vast unanimous sigh as it saw the rock wall split. A webbing of fracture radiated from the dent. And for a long moment his head was socketed there. He was motionless. But Pollux had slipped away and was behind him, raising his own fist. He pivoted on the soles of his feet and smashed his knuckles into the black pelt just above the waist—a kidney punch that would kill an ordinary man.

Amycus turned slowly. He seemed unhurt. His nose was flatter than before, and his forehead was scratched. But a slowness had fallen upon him, muffling him. He raised his arms again, but slowly. Pollux's left hand climbed painfully into the air; with two fingers he lifted the king's chin in a weirdly intimate way. Then he swung his right fist again, planting his feet, turning on his ankles, whipping his body around with all the tensile power of his spine, all the suave strength of his shoulders, all his hot love of battle and his cold loathing of the hairy brute who had been punishing him so.

His fist landed full on the king's throat. It was as if we were all attached now to that fist, could all feel the king's windpipe breaking under our knuckles.

Amycus stood there, swaying. Blood welled from every hole in his face, from his nostrils, his ears, his mouth. He tried to say something but only blew a bubble of blood. He fell face down on the trampled grass, and everyone knew he would never rise again.

T W E N T Y

E ACH YEAR, UPON THE NIGHT of the first full moon after the spring
sowing, the women of Colchis performed their rain dance. The
moon would rise slowly, beckoning a mob of wives to follow it
up the mountain. Among the leaping, shrieking women
walked a young man. Wearing a pair of gilded horns, clad in the
Golden Fleece, he strutted up the slope.

He had reason to be proud. Was he not the best athlete of the year,
winner of the long race, high jump, spear-throwing? Had he not been
chosen Rainmaker, Horned Man, Wearer of the Fleece? Was he not
being taken to the mountaintop to be loved by the seven most beautiful wives?

Then, after the last embrace, would not the sacred knives cut the
heart cleanly from his body before age could slacken his muscles or
blotch his hide? Should he not die in the flame of youth, giving his
blood to the furrows? And then, unhoused by the knives, would not
his potent ghost spin up into the low sky and freshen the cow-
goddess, whose milk is rain? No wonder he walked proudly among

the women, who leaped about him waving their knives and trying to kiss his shoulders as he went.

On that night, also, the maidens of Colchis climbed the mountain by another path and scattered about the lake shore, crouching there between two moons. For to look upon the moon in the water that night was to see the face of the man you would marry. If you had prayed ardently and otherwise pleased the goddess, you would see the drowning moon become the face of the young stranger who, from that night on, would inhabit your dreams.

The princess knelt on the shore, gazing up at the trees. She would see no moon mirrored in the lake, she knew, until it had untangled itself from the branches of tallest cedar and floated clear. As she watched the light trembling in the branches, she heard voices singing:

> *"You Hags of Heaven*
> *Number seven;*
> *Harpies favor hell . . .*
> *But when the Horned Man*
> *Mounts the Moon,*
> *You all come here to dwell."*

And that was where she wanted to be, among the wives, wild with summer, singing the moon out of the cedar and into the sky as they danced on the mountaintop.

But to do that, she had to be a wife herself.

Just then she saw light staining the water. The moon appeared very bright and solid, as if it had not dived into the lake but had swum up from the bottom. She stared at it. It paled under her gaze and began to wobble. Its edges melted into golden flame. Her breath caught in

her throat. The moon shook itself into pieces of golden light; they swam together and made a face.

She looked at it. It looked at her. The light blinded her eyes. Blackness swarmed. She didn't fall. She knelt there at the edge of the lake, unconscious but erect, hands digging into clay. When she opened her eyes, the moon was gone. She arose and turned from the lake.

"Stand where you are, Medea," said a voice.

"Who's that?"

"Aphrodite."

"Where are you?"

"Don't try to find me. If you were to look upon me now, you would burn to ashes."

"Show yourself, please. I don't turn to ashes so easily. I'm not sure I believe in you."

"Gently, child. Have I not just shown you your husband-to-be?"

"All I saw was a blob. Do you expect me to fall in love with that?"

"We are not speaking of love now but of marriage. You are a princess, the only daughter of a rich and powerful king. He wants a husband for you who will add to that wealth and power."

"And you call yourself the goddess of love."

"Get yourself married, girl. The work will prepare you for pleasure."

"Who is he?"

"Diomedes III, exiled king of Iolcus, otherwise known as Jason."

"Is he handsome?"

"Not bad. Rather small."

"Shorter than me?"

"Medea, my child, it doesn't matter if he's an absolute dwarf if he has a big army and a fat treasury. Have you not heard that I myself, Aphrodite, whose domain is love and beauty, took the ugliest and most misshapen of the gods in marriage? Nor did I weep and moan on my wedding night; I made him happy. And he has proved very kind and indulgent—and very, very rich."

"What you must understand, Goddess, is that I don't want to be a wife at all. I want to be a witch. I'm just learning magic now, just feeling my powers. I don't want to start thinking about a husband, rich or poor."

"Choice has been taken from you. You are destined to marry Jason and bear his child. I advise you to make the best of it, because the worst can be very, very bad."

"When do I meet him?"

"He's sailing here with a band of warriors. He's coming for the Fleece."

"My father will kill him."

"Then you won't have to marry him, will you?"

"I really don't understand you. You say one thing and seem to mean another. I don't know what to believe."

"Believe in me."

Her voice ceased.

"Aphrodite!"

"Farewell . . . "

"No! Don't go! Please." But the only thing Medea heard was an owl crying its hunger. "Aphrodite, Aphrodite, where are you? Come back!"

Silence. The women on the hilltop had stopped singing. She heard the lilt of water and the wind among the reeds. A rustle, a thump, a tiny scream; and she knew the owl had hit a field mouse. But she kept listening. There was something about the stillness that told her she was not alone.

Indeed she was not. Someone was very near, lying in the shadow of the embankment, half in the water, half out. It was a naiad who had come to the lake by underground streams to watch the rain dance. Climbing out, she had seen Medea kneeling so still there, watching for the drowned moon, so she had watched, too.

She saw the moon's reflection becoming a face, immediately fell in love with it, and waited there hoping it would appear in the water again. And when Aphrodite slid down a moonbeam to speak to the princess, she was there. And was still there when Aphrodite left.

Who was this creature?

Her name was Lethe. She was a water nymph, one who dwelt in lake and river and fountain. She had yellow hair and huge velvety black eyes. She looked like the kind of golden pansy that resembles a cat and is one of earth's most charming flowers. She swam like an otter and could run over a meadow without bending a blade of grass. And she had a fault that made her popular: what she was told by day, she forgot when the sun set; what she was told at night, she forgot by dawn. So she was much in demand by gods and mortals for telling secrets to. The secret most dangerous to tell is exactly the one you must tell—and who better for telling it to than one who listens with such wonder, widening her black eyes until you feel you could drown in them, and promptly forgets whatever she hears?

Long-legged laughing Lethe, the mischievous nymph of the for-getful ways, was much pursued because of her beauty, but rarely caught, and never kept. She had not yet found anyone she could really love—until this night when she had seen the face in the water. Now she was boiling with hot golden light, brimming with an enormous joy. She climbed the bank to stand before Medea.

"Aphrodite!" cried the girl.

"No, I am not Aphrodite."

"But she was just here . . . and she goes bare, with yellow hair. You must be she."

"Very flattering," said Lethe. "But I'm someone else. My name is Lethe, and I came out of that lake."

"Did you hear what she was telling me?"

"I did."

"I'm so confused. I don't know what to do," said Medea.

"There is one key to everything Aphrodite does these days. She wants that boy for herself."

"Jason?"

"Yes."

"But she's twice his size."

"She likes them small sometimes."

"How do you know about this?"

"How should I not? We nymphs gossip ceaselessly. What you think are leaves rustling are dryads whispering. What you think are gulls hunting are nereids shrieking the news. And what we gossip about, dear princess, is who wants whom and what they're doing about it. And we all know that Aphrodite still mourns the loss of Adonis, gored to death by Ares when he took the shape of a wild boar. Now she has been making plans for this Jason, who looks very much like Adonis. She chose him while he was still a green sprout, hiding him away on Cythera, and chaperoning him with platoons of witches. Now that he has leaped into manhood and is out voyaging, she hovers near his ship and attends his landfalls."

"Why, then, did she show me his face in the water? Why does she want me to marry him? She kept saying so. Why? Why?"

"I can think of one reason. He's coming here to claim the Golden Fleece. Your father, naturally, will attempt to kill him and his entire company. Perhaps Aphrodite thinks that, if you marry Jason, you will be able to protect him from your father's wrath."

"Did you see his face in the water?"

"Everyone sees someone different—the one she's destined to marry. But I don't go in for marriage much. I think it's selfish."

Lethe was babbling, lying when she remembered to, but getting mixed up and sometimes telling the truth. She was so happy she hardly knew what she was saying. A chorus of full-voiced shrieking drifted down from the mountaintop.

"They're hunting now," whispered Medea.

The chorus changed, narrowed to a single voice, screaming—a man's.

"They have him now. Time for the knives."

The shrieking fell to a moan, melted into the night wind, became an owl's cry. The moon was high and growing pale. It was striped by a red shadow.

"He's caught her," said Medea. "His shadow is upon her. We shall have rain."

"There's blood on the moon, Medea, and you cast a red shadow. Your eyes are a hawk's eyes full of cold yellow light. You are apt for sorcery and belong to the night."

"I know . . . I know . . . but Aphrodite says I must be wife, not witch."

"You can be both," said Lethe. "Many are. Farewell."

She dived into the lake and swam away underwater, murmuring, "I'll save him from that witch. I don't know how, but I will. Oh, Jason, Jason . . . I must be in love. I remember his name."

T W E N T Y - O N E

ETHE WAS FOLLOWING the *Argo*. She mingled with a school of dolphins and frisked about the ship so that she could gaze upon Jason without being seen.

"How can I make him love me?" she asked herself. "How do I contend against Aphrodite, Queen of Love and Beauty, and a hundred princesses of the Middle Sea, and shoals of nereids and naiads and dryads? How can I make him choose me, just me, among all these frantic females? I must make my move, or he'll get to Colchis and be gobbled up by that sullen witch."

In the meantime, she felt so wonderful and strong and swift swimming in the sparkling sea, watching her gray-eyed boy, that she laughed with joy. Then she ducked under, because she saw Jason look about as if he had heard her laughter.

"Trouble with me," she thought, "is I don't know how to worry. I'd better learn. No, I don't want to. People are always falling in love with me . . . so maybe this one will."

Indeed, even as she was thinking these things, this joyous nymph was being fallen in love with by someone she had never met. And a considerable someone. She couldn't see him now because he wore a cape of clouds and flew too high. But he was a great, brawling, black-bearded fellow with enormous powers. With one whisk of his cape he could sweep whole cities into the sea and capsize their fleets. He could fly to the top edge of the earth, fill his lungs, and come back and blow his breath over a warm place, turning rain into snow, freezing lakes and rivers, locking the earth in ice. He was the eldest son of Aeolus; he was Boreas, the North Wind.

He had been flying over the Middle Sea when he spotted the *Argo* and saw the beautiful naiad frisking about it and had fallen in love with her with all the desperate strength of his nature, which was fire under ice. He did not swoop down. He flew high, watching her. With a sure jealous instinct he guessed that she was following the ship for the sake of one of its crew, and he wanted to know which one. He vowed to himself that once he found out he would simply whisk his rival off the deck and hurl him to the bottom of the sea.

Boreas kept watching. He studied the big blond Twins especially. He studied redheaded Rufus swinging his sledge at his deck anvil; and Autolycus, who walked like a cat and might attract a cat-faced nymph; and iron-fanged Idas, fierce-looking enough to fascinate someone who liked to be frightened. But he took no special notice of Jason, who was one of the youngest aboard and among the smallest.

Then he saw Jason riding atop the mast, saw Lethe flash out of the water and float briefly on her back, hair floating. And he knew whom she wanted.

His gusty roar filled the sky. His black cape spread over the sky as he dived. He no longer wished to drown Jason. He wanted the pleasure of killing him with his hands. He meant to snap the mast in two, then impale him on the splintered end.

But even as he swooped, watching the crew scurry about to drop sail before the approaching squall, he realized that if he killed the boy before the nymph's eyes, she would never forgive him and never

love him. That thought made him postpone the pleasures of murder—but not for long, he vowed. He slowed his dive, leveled off, and
swooped away, leaving the sky clear. But he kept following the ship,
trying to think of a way to kill Jason without appearing to.

He was still hovering invisibly as the ship moored off a small island and the crew rowed ashore. They filled their water kegs quickly,
but couldn't bear to go aboard so soon. They enjoyed the feeling of
land beneath their feet.

They began to play. The Twins sparred. Autolycus tussled with
Rufus. Idas stuck a chock of wood on his spike to blunt it, and fenced
with Jason, who used a short sword. Ekion walked along the beach
with Daphnis. Argos, who never left the ship, was still aboard.

They raced. Autolycus won easily, Jason was second. They unslung their bows and shot at a mark. Jason won, shooting left-
handed. They threw spears. Castor and Pollux each won twice. Rufus
delighted himself by winning once. Then he produced a discus he
had forged. The discus then was a weapon, a solid polished disk of
metal with an edge so sharp it could shear through a medium-sized
tree. It could slice through the breast armor of a chariot horse and kill
the animal in full stride. Because of its sharp circular edge, you had
to wear a glove made of oxhide, sewn with linked metal.

As the young men sported in the sunlight, they had an audience of
two, though they didn't know it. Lethe had swum ashore and was
hiding in the pure-water stream, watching Jason. But she was aware
of the others. It was richly satisfying to see this lithe youth moving
among his magnificent shipmates. She could barely stop herself from
rushing out of the water to embrace him.

But, Boreas, also, was watching—and growing angrier and more
jealous as he watched, feeling himself fill with such gusty spite that
he had to clutch the tops of the towering cedars to stop himself from
diving upon the island and blowing them all into the sea. When they

began throwing the discus, his eyes kindled and an evil smile twisted his lips.

He watched Castor crouching and spinning and uncoiling—his torso gleaming as the heavy discus whirled away from his hand and flew and sheared through a pine tree. Pollux put on the glove, retrieved the discus, crouched and spun, and hurled it exactly as far as his twin had, slicing through a tree exactly as thick.

Rufus put on the glove. All the contestants stood behind the thrower. But Boreas was watching only Jason. An idea had flared suddenly in the cavern of his mind. He studied the forest below until he found a hollow tree and blew softly into its bole, making a moaning sound.

Daphnis looked up, startled. Jason turned completely and searched the forest, trying to see where the sound had come from. Boreas blew again, softly. Again that moaning call. And Boreas didn't breathe again until he saw Jason, obeying the impulse of leadership, move off from the others and walk across the clearing toward the woods just as Rufus whirled and sent the discus flying through the air.

Boreas, who had been holding his breath, spat it out in a great spiteful gust, catching the discus as it sailed, holding it in a grip of air, and hurling it back straight at Jason's head.

Lethe screamed, unheard. Everyone stood frozen, watching the glittering death whirl toward the boy—all except Pollux. He leaped into the air, arms outstretched, hands cupped—and fell to earth, spouting blood as the spinning blade passed through flesh and bone and sinew, cutting off both hands at the wrist. For a moment, all froze.

Then it was Jason who became a blur of action, plastering mud on Pollux's stumps, and tying them off to stop the bleeding. Lethe, watching from the stream, saw how war and war games had honed

these young men to move in a cool ballet of efficiency though their hearts were breaking. They brought Pollux gently and swiftly into the skiff, slid it into the surf, and made it fly over the water toward the *Argo*.

Lethe floated near, watching. She saw Rufus light the forge fire and heat a sword blade red hot. Jason led Pollux to the anvil. The Spartan, pale and tottering now, but trying to hold himself erect, and clenching his jaws so that he wouldn't moan, placed his stumps on the anvil. Rufus laid the flat of the red-hot blade on the torn flesh. Boreas, hovering invisibly, snuffed up the smoke as if it were the savor of dinner cooking. For he hated all the crew now, especially this one who had thwarted his attempt to kill Jason. "I'll get him next time," he muttered.

Jason was watching Pollux very closely. The stumps had been sealed by fire. But now, the hours after, was the critical time when he might die from shock and blood loss. Castor sat on the deck, pillowing his twin's head on his lap, stroking his brow. Pollux's face was white as bone.

Suddenly he spoke—not in his usual rumble but in a small voice, very clear, as if the thoughts were drifting in their purity out of his mouth.

"Lucky day," he said.

His friends looked at one another swiftly. They thought he was raving. He spoke again: "Idas, Idas, ugly Idas, now I know, meat must go. Spike hands, brass choppers, you've shown me something, man. Amputation is opportunity. I'm ready, ready, for retooling. Rufus, my friend, make me a pair of iron hands I can close into iron fists—and do a few other things with."

Lethe wept as she listened, feeling very odd. Naiads, whose faces are always wet, rarely weep because they can't taste the tears.

Jason spoke one word: "Rufus."

Rufus leaped to the top of the anvil. He was naked to the waist and streaked with soot. He had grown since coming to sea. Shoulders and chest bulged massively now under a pelt of red hair. He raised his arms to the sky, and cried, "Great Hephaestus, I call to you! Lend me a spark of your divine fire. Rich you are among the gods, snatching fat marrow from the very bones of earth—copper and tin and good brown iron. Lavish are the gifts you make: magic mirror for your mother, Hera; bracelets and necklaces for beautiful Thetis; a flying ax for Ares. Here today we have seen one mortal more generous than god has ever dared: a man who lives by his hands giving both of them to save his friend—rewarded with agonizing pain, helplessness, perhaps death. You heard what he asks, my lord. Now guide my tools. Teach me to make metal hands, hard for combat, gentle for love."

Thunder rumbled from a cloudless sky—like sledges pounding a far anvil. Lightning forked, stabbing into the deck hearth, kindling the piled charcoal.

Rufus shouted with joy. He sprang at his heap of metal, plucked out an iron bar, and plunged it into the flame. For the next twelve days and nights he worked ceaselessly at his anvil, needing no sleep, scarcely stopping to eat. A spark of the smith-god's vital fire had indeed lighted the tinder of his loyal heart, and he was laboring to save his friend. He produced a pair of metal hands. So cunningly did he fashion them, with nerve and ligature and sinew spun from the finest of platinum wire, that they would be able to perform the most delicate of manual tasks as well as the most brutal. When Pollux balled his iron hands into iron fists, there could be no man or demigod to stand against him—for Hercules was dead.

TWENTY-TWO

LETHE, WHO WAS TOLD so many secrets because she would immediately forget them, was a favorite at Aphrodite's court. Most secrets are love secrets and Aphrodite was always bursting with the latest one. So she was glad to greet Lethe.

"How nice to see you, my darling. But you're not your usual smiling self."

"I have a question, Queen of the Night."

"Yes, dear."

"It's about Jason the Argonaut. You used to fancy him."

"Still do."

"But you want him to marry Medea, it is said."

"Not to love her, though."

"Why must they marry, then?"

"To save his life. Unless he comes as Medea's husband, the king of Colchis will kill him. That's why I thought of this match. Anyway, it won't happen."

"Why not?"

"My son Eros, the Archer of Love, refuses to go to Colchis and shoot his arrow as I direct. And Medea simply won't feel a thing for

Jason unless Eros pierces her untried heart with one of his darts."

"And why won't he?"

"He's getting very bratty. Everyone spoils him. He won't do anything for me unless I bribe him. And I've run out of bribes."

"Shall I try to persuade him? In my own way."

"But why? What's your interest in the matter?"

"I've glimpsed the *Argo* as I've swum the sea. Some of those boys are gorgeous."

"What! You've fallen for Jason, too?"'

"Oh no!" cried Lethe, knowing it was better to lie. "Not Jason. But if he's killed in Colchis, the rest of the crew are doomed. And there's a pair of twins aboard—"

"Ah yes, the Twins! Which one do you fancy?"

"I don't know. I'd never be able to remember which is which, anyway. So I'd like to save them both to make sure. Which means saving Jason first. Which means Eros will have to go shoot Medea."

"Is this my giddy, forgetful Lethe? You're being so logical."

"Well, in an emergency. Actually, I like to think now and then. But it's hard to start. May I go work on your son?"

"Any way you like. And if you get him to do this, I shall be eternally grateful."

"I may have occasion to remind you of that one day. Farewell."

She ran off. Aphrodite watched her admiringly. Lethe had long legs and ran very swiftly, yellow hair floating. She was running because she had seen Eros playing in the meadow as she came, and she wanted to catch him.

She found him in the meadow, playing with the latest toy his mother had bribed him with—a round polished sapphire, large as a tennis ball. When tossed in the air, it left a trail of fire, as if it were a piece of broken star. He tossed the sapphire and watched in delight as it branded the air with blue fire, then fell.

It never reached his hand. Another hand, at the end of a long arm, had snatched the gem from the air. Eros looked up and saw a nymph towering above him, pinning his sapphire into her yellow hair.

"Give me that!"

"Hello, Eros."

"Oh, Lethe, give me my sapphire. I don't like anyone else playing with it."

"But it looks so nice in my hair." She plucked an arrow from his quiver, held it by its point, and swished it through the air.

"What are you doing? Give that back."

"Oh, you'll be getting it, never fear."

Lethe reached her long arm and lifted him like an infant, tucking him under her arm back to front. She struck him a whistling blow with the arrow. He shrieked.

"Stop! Stop! Put me down."

She sat on a log and stood him on the ground between her knees. "Do you know what I'm probably going to do now?"

"Don't! Please."

"Oh, but I probably will. What's going to happen, most likely, is that I'm going to turn you over my knee and give you the spanking of your life with your own arrow. What you got before was just a taste."

"No ... no ... "

"But you deserve it. You've been very naughty—disobeying your mother, neglecting your chores. You're sadly in need of correction."

"Please let me go, Lethe."

"Why should I?"

"I'm not to be made to suffer pain, not ever. It's cosmically incorrect."

"It is, now?"

"Please ... somebody may see us."

"Everyone will. I'll call the dryads from the trees and whistle the naiads out of the fountain, and they'll all come to watch. They'll enjoy it."

"Won't you let me go? What do you want me to do?"

"Obey your mother. Go to Colchis and shoot Medea with one of your arrows, making her fall in love with Jason the Argonaut."

"All right, I will. Now let me go."

"Not quite yet. Hold still. I want you to explain something to me. There seem to be two kinds of arrows in your quiver, one kind with golden points, the other with silver."

"Not silver, that's lead. They're the arrows of indifference. Let me go. You're squeezing the breath out of me."

"Tell me about the arrows. Slowly and clearly. I'm getting impatient."

"Well, you know about the golden ones: whoever I shoot with one of those falls in love with someone standing near. But another venom spreads when I pierce someone with the leaden arrow. What fills the heart then is not love, but icy indifference."

"But you do have different kinds of love arrows for different kinds of love? There is a love that lasts a lifetime, and beyond. There is love that lasts only till dawn. And there is love that changes to hate."

"All done with the same arrows. But I have different ways of shooting."

"Aha, I thought so. What I want you to do is this: shoot Medea with a golden arrow and make her love Jason, but with a love that will not last."

She had stretched her legs while speaking, and he slid away. She was on him in three strides. He felt himself being plucked off the grass and folded across her long thighs. One hand clamped him there.

"No . . . no . . . " he yelped. "Please."

She dug her fingers into his flesh and twisted in a slow pinch. "Owww . . . "

"If you scream like that now, what will you sound like when I've been smacking your divine little bottom for an hour or two?"

"I give up. Completely. I'll do whatever you want."

"Are you sure you know what I want?"

"I'm to go to Colchis and shoot my arrow into Medea, making her fall in love with Jason with a love that will change to hate."

"Can I trust you?"

"You have to. I'm the only one who can do it."

"Tell me exactly how you'll go about it."

"I'll shoot Medea with a golden arrow as she's looking at Jason. Immediately afterward, I'll shoot Jason with a leaden arrow of indifference. She'll love him till they're married, and for a time thereafter. But when her love meets his indifference, it will turn to hate."

"Hearken, Eros: if you betray me, if you fail to do what you've promised, or do something else, I'll search the world for you. I'll find you wherever you are and after I finish with you, you won't even be able to sit down on a cloud."

"May I go now?"

She lifted him off her lap. They looked at each other. She was very beautiful. She suddenly bent and kissed him on the lips. He smiled. He was the godling of love, after all; his flesh was magical. To touch him was to risk enslavement, which was really why Aphrodite had never dared punish him. And he knew he had awakened something in Lethe that would never sleep again.

T W E N T Y - T H R E E

THE ARGONAUTS LANDED BY NIGHT on the wild coast of Colchis. The black ship slipped silently into a little cove; the men disembarked and pulled it ashore. They held council on the beach under the moon.

"We are too few to do it by force," said Jason. "So we must hide our intention under a cloak of diplomacy. Four of us will visit the castle: Ekion, myself, and two volunteers. The rest of you will remain here, in hiding, until such time as we reappear with or without the Fleece. We shall then hold counsel again and make final plans."

"You'll have no chance to practice diplomacy," said Argos. "King Aetes will lop off your heads as soon as he lays eyes on you. He will kill you and then send troops to search inlet and cove. We shall be found, we shall be slaughtered. And the ship, my beautiful ship, will burn."

"Less talk and more action," growled Castor. "This quest is turning into a debating society. I've had no chance at all to break any necks. If you're going to the castle, I'm going with you. I suppose that's what you mean by volunteering. My brother volunteers, too."

"Yes," said Pollux. "I haven't had any chance to test my new fists."

"*Our* new fists," said Rufus. "I should be going with you, too, Jason."

"Sorry," said Jason. "Three is all I can take this time. But I think I can promise every one of you all the action you'll want."

Some hours later, it appeared as though the shipwright's gloomy hunch were to come true. Before Aetes' throne stood Jason, Ekion, Castor, and Pollux, manacled with thick chains and hemmed about with heavily armed warriors of the royal guard. Aetes sat on a high throne made of ivory and jade. He was a squat, vicious-looking man. His robe was a pelt taken from the rare white polar wolf. His crown was of red gold inlaid with the teeth of the same wolf. But it was his daughter who occupied Jason.

Medea sat at the foot of the throne. Jason, studying her, saw a very tall woman, sleek and muscular in her short linen tunic, with huge yellow eyes and a mane of black hair. He was fascinated by her hands. They were beautifully shaped with very long fingers, but instead of fingernails they were tipped with ripping talons like a hawk's.

"You have come to take my Fleece," said Aetes. "So I shall take your heads—which seems eminently fair."

"Indeed, O King," said Ekion. "All the civilized world marvels at your instinct for equity. So you should recognize that we do not come here to steal the Fleece, but in honorable embassy, seeking to arrange a transfer. It was stolen from our ancestors, after all, by your ancestors. Naturally, we would be prepared to make a contribution to the upkeep of its shrine."

"Honorable embassy, eh?" said Aetes. "Is that why you steal ashore like thieves in the night and leave your crew hiding on the beach while you come here to spy out our position? No, my friends, you are not ambassadors but thieves, thieves and spies. Now you,

Jason, your snake-tongued herald, and your two Spartan thugs must pay for your folly with your heads."

It was now that Eros came to them. He flew into the throne room just as the king was pronouncing sentence, notched an arrow, and shot it into the heart of Medea. The whole performance was invisible.

Medea felt a strange sweet pain stabbing into her chest. Now, she dabbled in witchcraft, was acquainted with spells, enchantments, and other magical effects—but for all her experience she could not believe what was happening to her. It was as if a membrane had been peeled from her vision. She saw the world all new. And the main fact of this new world was a condemned prisoner, a boyish pirate with black hair and gray eyes who bore his chains with such dignity. Suddenly she saw him as a pillar of rosy fire casting a fragrance that almost made her swoon. The sparks of this fire entered all her tender places and made her burn with agonizing sweetness. She wanted to dig her claws into him softly, lick his blood like honey, feast on his mouth. She wanted to be all the women he had ever known—mother, nurse, sister, wife, slave—daughter if he had one.

The soldiers of the guard laid hands on the chains, preparing to lead the prisoners away. Medea uncoiled her full length and raised her voice in a blood-chilling falcon shriek. It stopped all sound, all movement in the huge throne room. All eyes swung to her.

"O great Aetes, Father and King, I am weary of executions."

The king frowned. "What is your meaning, princess? Would you pardon these thieves?"

"Not at all. But beheadings grow monotonous. Let us gain some entertainment from their punishment."

"Entertainment? What do you suggest?"

"The Marriage Task."

The king's scowl deepened. The courtiers gasped. For the Marriage Task was an outmoded rite. In times past, it had been the sacred ordeal to be undergone by anyone who aspired to wed a princess of Colchis. It was centuries old, but in Medea's time it was used not as a courtship rite but to rid the king of any suitor he considered undesirable. And Aetes was surprised now that Medea had thought of this robber as a suitor, even if she meant him to die in the arena.

"Do you consider this Jason a candidate for your hand, O daughter?"

"I consider him a candidate for Hades, O Father. I am proposing that he be dispatched to those dark precincts by the Brass Bulls."

"Very well," said Aetes. "We shall forgo the chopping block for these young men, although I think it would be much simpler. Take them to the dungeon. They face the Brass Bulls tomorrow."

TWENTY-FOUR

J ASON LAY UNCOMFORTABLY ASLEEP in his tiny stone dungeon. He dreamed that he was bound like Prometheus to a crag, and that a huge sleek black bird with a woman's face was diving at him, claws extended. He awoke to find Medea bending over him.

"You will be more comfortable without the chains," she said. She pointed to the manacles, muttering. They dropped from him like strands of seaweed.

"Thank you, Princess."

"Yes, you have much to be grateful for. Had it not been for me, your headless body would now be ripening on the midden."

"I know how much I owe you," said Jason. "Perhaps my performance tomorrow may provide you with sufficient entertainment to pay some small part of my debt."

"Your performance tomorrow, and that of your companions, will last precisely as long as the wink of an eye, my dear pirate, unless special arrangements are made on your behalf. The monsters you will face come out of the smithy of Daedalus. They are giant bulls cast in brass, made by the arch-mechanic as instruments of war for his master, Minos, and purchased by my father after Minos died.

Their horns can shear through any substance. They can charge through a stone wall ten feet thick and come out the other side without a dent. But they will not have to touch you with their horns or their razor hooves. For their breath is of fire. They spit flame. At the distance of a mile they can ignite a whole forest, or, with exquisite marksmanship, burn the bark off a sapling and leave the trunk unmarked. All those who have entered the arena with them have been incinerated."

"Now, truly," said Jason, "my companions and I would seem to need these special arrangements you mention."

"You must anoint yourself with this unguent," she said, giving him a small crystal flask. "It is made of the tears that Io wept after she was changed into a cow and tormented by Hera's gadfly. And these tears are mixed with fat rendered from the salamander that lives in flame and from certain essences of the phoenix, that marvelous bird that dies in flame but is resurrected therein. Spread this salve upon you from head to foot, and have your companions do likewise. Then the fiery breath of the bulls will play about you as harmlessly as the evening breeze."

"I shall spread the salve," said Jason. "What else must I do?"

"Nothing. The bulls will become confused when they see you unscathed by the flame. They will panic, and turn upon each other, breathing fire, and be turned thereby into pools of molten brass."

"Indeed, dear lady, how shall I ever be able to thank you?"

"Oh, you will have a lifetime to think of ways," said Medea. "This ordeal is a Marriage Task. You will be the first to have passed it. Why do you furrow your brow, O successful suitor? Do you find the prospect of marriage with me so displeasing?"

Jason looked at her. She was formidably tall in the glare of moonlight that lanced through the slot in the dungeon wall. She seemed to grow taller as he watched. Medea had the weirdly limitless quality of those who work in magic. He did not know how to estimate her; she was without frontiers. The idea of "too much" was at the marrow of her manner. She stood there before him, alert and powerful as a predatory bird. She lifted her long arm and softly raked his cheek with her claws. He concealed his shudder behind a smile. She was the hawk girl who had visited his sleep; she had no wings now but was otherwise the same. Had she known she was waiting for him? He took her hand and examined it, turned it over, and kissed its palm.

"Sharp claws," he murmured. "I shall have to file them down." She took the flask from him. "Let me anoint you, fiancé."

At first it all went as Medea had promised. The Brass Bulls, each larger than an elephant, stood pawing the ground, glittering in the sunlight, as the dense swarm of onlookers began a low, seething murmur like the wind in grass. The bulls spotted the three young men standing in the arena; they shook their horns and leveled their heads. Twin jets of fire spurted from their brass nostrils.

Jason believed in Medea's magic, but it was all he could do to stand there pretending no fear as the brazen beasts spat flame. He stood between Castor and Pollux, a hand on the arm of each. He felt their massive arms quivering and clasped them more tightly, whispering, "Show them." The ancients believed in appearances. They believed that outward manner revealed inner quality, that the weakness that was not indulged could be transformed into a strength.

So the young Hellenes stood awaiting fire.

The amazed crowd saw them continue to stand there, arm in arm, smiling, unconsumed in the very heart of flame. Jason left the others and vaulted over the railing into the royal box, where sat Aetes and Medea. He bowed to the king and knelt before Medea—who raised a wand and touched him on each eye, the mouth, and the knees.

The willow wand turned into a snake in her hands, a mottled yellow and black serpent that cast itself into loops, swiftly and more swiftly twining, coiling, uncoiling, weaving itself into hypnotic patterns as Medea crooned a wordless song. Then the snake was a rope braiding and unbraiding itself in Medea's hands. The rope became a garland of red and purple flowers that Medea twisted into a wreath and placed on Jason's head. All Jason's attention and the focus of the crowd had been turned from what was happening in the arena and were caught up in the sleepy maze of snake and rope and garland.

But there is always a level of a hero's awareness that cannot be lured from the business at hand, especially when the business is fighting. Something broke into Jason's trance and pulled his eyes away from Medea's magic. He abruptly looked up and saw what was happening in the arena.

When his gaze pierced the dust, he realized that his bride-to-be was acting treacherously. The Brass Bulls had not turned upon each other as she had promised—but, seeing Castor and Pollux unconsumed by flame, were charging in to finish them off with horn and hoof. When Jason saw them they were in mid-charge, galloping with such terrific speed that he had no chance of intervening, but had to stand by helplessly and watch the Twins being destroyed.

A hideous clanging shattered the air as metal crashed on metal—and Jason, amazed, overjoyed, saw Pollux punching great dents into the Brass Bull with his iron fists. Iron is harder than brass, and the Spartan was fired by a gleeful battle rage. His shoulders bunched with muscle; he swung his arms like sledges. The huge iron mauls that were his fists crashed again and again into the beast, knocking off its horns, flattening its face, pounding it into a shapeless mass of metal.

Castor had seized the horns of the other bull and, straining his thews until he thought they must burst his skin, was slowly twisting the monster's brass head around. Finally he wrenched it off with a

bell-like sound, turned, and tossed the head to Jason in the Royal Box. Jason caught it and offered it to Medea, saying, "A souvenir of your treachery, Princess."

"I meant no treachery, husband."

"Liar! Witch! You are no wife of mine!"

"I saved you from the bulls."

"And sought to betray my friends."

"All for love of you. They are your friends, and I am jealous. I am jealous of everyone you ever spoke to, smiled upon. I am jealous of the ground you walk on, the clothes you wear. I am nothing now but my ravenous love for you, and that love has turned into a pestilence in my veins."

"This marriage of ours promises to be dangerous for my friends," said Jason.

"You are a king. You need no friends."

"I am a battle chief. I lead men. I love those I go into battle with. If I keep you as my wife, you must exempt my companions from your malice."

"You are the master. I am your slave."

She was unused to begging for anything; the strangeness of it made her look younger, vulnerable, very beautiful in her gown of black and gold with diamonds twined in her black mane. And Jason, gazing at her, felt a strange power rising within him. Again he had that sense of Medea's excess, knew that she would be as extreme in surrender as she could be potent in conflict, and that she would lead him through corridors of feeling that few had walked before.

"Forgive me," she whispered.

"Lead me to the Golden Fleece and help me bear it away."

"Your quest is my quest, husband. My father's goods are my dowry."

T W E N T Y - F I V E

ON THE FIFTH DAY AFTER THEIR WEDDING, he asked her to keep her promise and lead him to the Fleece.

"Lord husband," she said, "I am mindful of my vow, but the time is not yet."

"In matters perilous," he said, "the time is always now. Hesitation breeds doubt, doubt breeds fear. Fear breeds failure."

"Ah, my prince, I have seen you in action and know what you can do. No one is so ready for daring deed as you; no one more apt to pluck glory from the very jaws of terror. But the perils that surround the Golden Fleece lie beyond your experience. They belong to a different order of event. This relic is tainted by an ancient curse."

"I don't understand."

"But I do. This matter belongs to the realm of dire enchantment—to which I, as priestess of Hecate, have learned certain clues. In an attempt to find the luckiest date for taking the Fleece, I have considered the flight of cranes and the entrails of doves. I have cast numbers, deciphered the path of certain falling stars, sifted salamander ash, and done other readings I am not permitted to divulge, even to you. And they all say the same thing: the months ahead are swollen with evil omen. Your voyage here and your adventures on the way, your successful combat with the Brass Bulls have used up your credit with the gods. You must abide here quietly with me and attempt no adventure until your luck ripens again."

"How long will that be?"

"More than a year, say the portents. At least a year and a day. For another kind of fortune has begun to ripen. You have planted a child in me. It is written that you must see that child, and that child must learn to know you, before you risk your life again."

He smiled and took her in his arms. "We shall prepare a mighty welcome for the little prince or princess," he said. "But after a year and a day, you must lead me to the Fleece."

"I will. I swear."

For some months Jason and Medea lived peaceably as husband and wife, and he tried to love her. But Eros had pierced his heart with the leaden arrow of indifference, and he could not respond to her passion. He kept pretending but grew very restless. He hated living in the palace. He felt his sword rusting and his youth growing stale. He ached to be at sea again, being blown toward adventure.

Then, one night, Lethe came.

She swam, unseen, into an arm of the river that cut through the palace grounds. This was the night she meant to meet him. She couldn't wait any longer. She climbed the bank and began to sing.

Jason was in his chamber, sleeping. He awoke suddenly. He heard a voice singing, very faint and far away. Faint as it was, it threaded its way through other sounds, and he knew he had to arise and follow it into the night. Medea was not there. This did not surprise him. She arose often to prowl the castle grounds.

So he thought he might meet her when he entered the park, but

none of the shadows hardened into his wife. The voice was singing. He followed it through the garden and through an orchard, to the riverbank. He could hear the words now:

"Come to the river
Where love runs deep.
Do not give her
Your heart to keep."

"Who's there?" he called. The voice kept singing.

"Down, down,
Out of sight.
Drown, drown,
In green-gold light."

"Who's there?"
He heard laughter.
"Answer me!"
"My name is Lethe."
Naked and dripping, she arose before him. Her hair was moon-brown, but he knew it would be yellow by day. He couldn't tell the color of her eyes because they were full of moonlight.
"Lethe . . . is that your name?"
"Yes. And you are Janus."
"Jason."
"Oh yes, Jason. I'm quite forgetful. Especially about names."
"I suppose everybody tells you you're beautiful."
"Not quite everybody. But I don't mind hearing it again. Not at all."
"You're beautiful."

"Want to go swimming?"

She grasped his hand and dived in, pulling him after her. He swam superbly for a mortal, but she was a dolphin in the water. He tried to harmonize his strokes with hers; she slowed for him, and they swam in a dreamy kind of ballet under the moon.

"You're a pretty good swimmer," she said.

"Not like you."

"Oh well . . . I'm a naiad. Shall we go under?"

"Underwater?"

"You'll like it down there."

"I'll drown."

"I won't let you. I can breathe underwater. It's water that goes in but air that comes out; that's why fish blow bubbles. When I have mortal guests, I breathe for them."

"How?"

She flung her arms about him, put her lips to his, and blew into his mouth. "Like that."

"Are you sure it works underwater?"

"Always has."

"Let's go, then."

She held him around the waist as they sank. It was warmer than he had expected and not quite dark. Greenish moonlight sifted in. He was holding his breath as they slowly sank. His chest burned. She pressed his belly, and he felt the dead air leave his lungs. She immediately clasped him to her, put her mouth to his, and blew air into him.

It was better than air; it bubbled deep in his lungs. He felt his blood fizzing. The cares of the quest suddenly melted away. Weightless underwater, clasped in her smooth strong arms, drinking her breath, he felt this hour the flushing out of the foul memories of a marriage made for the wrong reasons.

He pulled his mouth from hers so he could kiss her shoulder, inhaled water, and began to choke. She pulled him to the surface half-drowned. He coughed and floundered. She dived and came up under him. He was riding her astride. She swam toward shore.

"Let me off."

"Oh, why?"

"We'll sink."

"Nonsense. You feel light as a feather. I could carry you across the sea this way. Are you comfortable?"

"Yes."

"Slide back a bit. Swing your legs up and rest your feet on my shoulders."

He did. He felt her sleek and warm beneath him, and marveled at her strength. He was resting comfortably; he felt her shoulder muscles sliding under his feet. By the time they reached shore he knew that the world had changed for him. He was dismayed to see torchlight—to hear shouting and laughter—and to find the ship's company on the bank, stripping to swim.

"Well met by moonlight!" called Daphnis. "Who's this enchanting creature? How can I be mad for her so soon? Introduce us immediately."

"I'm Lethe," she said.

"I'm Daphnis. Never mind the others."

"She's too big for you," said Castor. "She needs men of stature."

"Lethe . . . " said Daphnis. "Did he find you in the river?"

"I found him, little one. I came looking."

Jason introduced the crew to her, one by one. She kept laughing. "Never, never will I remember these names." She slid between Castor and Pollux and took an arm of each.

"Twins," she murmured. "Big beautiful ones. But we'd better not start anything. How would I ever remember which was which?"

Pollux held up his iron fists. "Only one of us has these. Me. My brother just has the old-fashioned kind."

"You don't want to get mixed up with those two," said Daphnis. "Double trouble all the way through. But consider this carefully: there's only one of me."

"Yes, consider him," said Ekion. "He's not as childish as he seems. A bit befuddled, perhaps, but he can handle it. He's a poet."

Idas and Autolycus were silent. They stood there in the spangled light, lean as wolves, staring at her. This amused the nymph. Mirth gripped her entire body. Her hair shook, her eyes shone, her teeth flashed, her long legs quivered.

"I love you all," she said. "Every one of you, large and small. But I've made my choice for now. So dive in, boys, and swim away."

"Would you, perchance, have any sisters in this river?" said Ekion.

"Half a shoal, which is seven, one for each. They're floating around in there, waiting for the party to start."

Shouting joyously, the crew dove in and swam away. Jason and Lethe stared at each other. They stood close; he was wrapped in her fragrance; they did not touch. She laughed softly.

"You mind that I'm so tall? Your wife is, too, isn't she?"

"That's the only resemblance."

"Good."

"Every way you are is the way I want you to be. I've never loved anyone before."

"Neither have I. And I've searched and searched. Tried this and that."

"I don't want to dance here. This is the royal garden. A blighted place. Let's go underwater."

"Shall you be able to stay under so long?"

"You'll teach me to breathe there. And perhaps I'll teach you to remember."

TWENTY-SIX

NOW, MEDEA HAD FOLLOWED HIM to the river, and stood there wrapped in shadow, watching him dance with Lethe. She watched them for hours, then returned slowly to her empty bed.

She did not sleep. Her eyes smoldered and her talons twitched; she felt that she must tear his heart from his chest and roast it for her dinner. But no, it was too soaked in treachery; it might poison her. She would toss it to the carp who swarmed in the castle pond and would eat anything.

By morning her rage had frozen into hatred. "Murder is too swift," she said to herself. "I need a slower, more painful vengeance." So she smiled when he came to her, and imitated tenderness, saying, "I have good news for you, husband. The omens have changed. The gods have allowed your luck to ripen, and it is suitable now for you to take the Fleece, if that is what you want."

"You know it is," he said. "And I rejoice that the time has come."

"I have not forgotten my promise," she said. "We were granted some months to love each other without fret, but now I am ready to guide you to the Fleece. Remember, though, that it is guarded by an enormous serpent that feeds on anything that moves, and can swallow an ox as a cat does a grasshopper."

"We'll go there alone," he said. "I want to take a good look at this monster before making plans."

She led him up the slope of the same wild mountain where the women did their rain dance . . . led him past the lake where she had first seen his face, up, up, past the timberline to where a stone temple stood. He heard a horrid mixture of sounds—rustling, grunting, slurping, thin screams—and saw a fawn being swallowed by a giant serpent. The fawn was going down head last; its eyes seemed to be begging Jason to help.

He couldn't bear the sight; he looked away. And saw that Medea was watching with glittering yellow eyes and a little smile. He knew then that he must leave her—but not until he had stolen the Fleece. He also knew he couldn't afford to be squeamish. He had come here to study something he would have to fight. He forced himself to keep watching as the serpent swallowed the fawn.

Now it saw them, began to slither toward them, opening its mouth. It was huge, Jason saw: twice the length of the *Argo* and as thick as the bole of a cedar.

"No weapon can pierce its hide," whispered Medea. "Not arrow, not spear." Indeed, Jason saw that its hide was of hard mottled leather, thick as armor. "When it flails its tail, it knocks down trees," said Medea.

"Isn't it getting rather close?" said Jason.

Medea whistled a two-noted birdcall. The serpent stopped slithering and began to rise, uncoiling, climbing the air, higher and higher, stretching its jaws until Jason thought it must be hinged at the tail. It was a hundred feet of living gullet, lined with teeth.

"Does it obey you?" he said.

"Only me," she said. "And only sometimes."

"Can you make it leave this place?"

"Some nights, I take it hunting. Down the slope, through the trees, to a place where the fawns dance. But it doesn't stay long. Brings its kill back."

"How long can I count on?"

"Two hours or so."

"Time enough. Will you take it hunting tomorrow night so that we can get into the temple?"

"What then? Will you sail away with the Fleece and leave me here?"

"Of course not. You'll meet me at the cove where the *Argo* lies hidden and sail with me to my kingdom."

The serpent stood on its tail now, undulating slightly, weaving its head. It was taller than the temple. Medea whistled again, three bars this time. The serpent lowered itself into coils and lay there motionless. Its eyes were lidless and could not close, but Jason knew it was not asleep.

"What did you tell it?" he said.

"That I'll come back in three nights and take it hunting."

"Why wait? Why not tomorrow night?"

"In three days, my father and his war chiefs will leave the city. They go to inspect the troops that guard our northern frontier. It will be better for you if the king and his captains are on the other side of the country when you steal the Fleece."

"Yes. You're a better tactician than I am, my dear."

"Kings' daughters are trained in deception, even before they become wives."

The lidless eyes watched them depart.

TWENTY - SEVEN

EKION

JASON SUMMONED US TO A FINAL MEETING before the raid, all of us except Argos, of course, who never left the ship. Upon the night appointed, we were to climb the mountain to the shrine of the Fleece. Medea would have gone before to lead the serpent away, leaving the place unguarded. Jason and Autolycus were to enter the temple and take the Fleece. The Twins, Idas, and Rufus were to patrol the clearing and kill anyone who approached, while Daphnis and I, the noncombatants, were to station ourselves in trees to give warning if anyone came near.

We rehearsed the march by day so that we could go torchless by night. We climbed the slope, but stopped short of the temple clearing.

"I don't want to disturb the serpent," said Jason. "And you're as well off not seeing it."

"How long will your wife keep it occupied?" I asked.

"Two hours, she says. Choose your tree now, so you won't have to search for it in the dark. You, too, Daphnis."

It was windy on the mountain that night; my tree swayed under me like a mast. I had to clench the bough with my knees as if I were

riding a horse. The moon flared briefly, then flared again, as if the wind were trying to blow it out. The sky must have been full of broken clouds. I was there to keep watch, but it was hard to read the shadows.

I heard something: sliding, rustling, then wetter sounds. And a mellow bleating sound, almost like a sob. I was staring my eyes out, but the wind had blown the moon away, and I saw nothing. The sounds grew closer. The moon flared. Then I saw . . .

I didn't want to believe it. It was something out of the very earliest legends—of chaos clotting into a giant life-blob that shaped itself into a giant snail. Here it was, returned, crawling out of the rubble of chaos, enormously long and thick, wearing horns. The moon rode a clear patch of sky. The thing was passing beneath, and I saw it plain. It was no snail. It was a gigantic serpent; in its jaws, half-engulfed, was a full-grown stag.

Then I did the bravest thing I had ever done: I screamed. My every impulse was to shrink so profoundly into the tree that I would become part of the bark. But I didn't. I screamed as loudly as I could to warn the others, even though I knew the thing below would be the first to hear.

It ignored my screaming. It passed my tree and moved into the clearing.

TWENTY-EIGHT

THE YOUNG MEN STOOD BEFORE the stone temple that was the shrine of the Fleece. Jason pushed at its heavy brass door; it didn't budge. Pollux closed his iron hand into an iron fist and pulled his arm back.

"No," said Jason. "Don't hit it. They'll hear the clanging in the palace."

"Maybe we can push it down," said Castor. "Let's put our shoulders to it."

But as they spoke, Autolycus had been tinkering with the bolt. The door swung open.

"Enter," said Autolycus.

Jason followed him in. The Twins stayed outside to patrol the clearing. Inside, Jason and Autolycus knelt to the ground when they saw the Fleece. It was larger than the *Argo*'s mainsail and seemed woven of the shifting lights of dawn, casting a dim radiance through the dark chamber.

"Truly a garment of the gods," said Jason. "Worthy of a hero's quest."

"We'd better roll it up," said Autolycus. "It shines in the dark."
Then they heard Ekion screaming.

They rushed out of the shrine and saw the serpent. It had coiled itself in a single loop around the temple and its garden. The six young men stood inside a rampart of living leather.

The monster was in no hurry. It was swallowing a stag. It had all the time there was to attend to those within its loop. The sky was clear now, and the moon was a torch. The Argonauts stood there enclosed by the monster. They heard sounds of swallowing.

"Perhaps he'll choke on the horns," said Jason. "I saw an anaconda do that once—on a goat's horns. But that was only an earthworm compared to this one."

He spoke calmly but he was scorching inside, suffocating with rage because he knew Medea had betrayed them and furious at himself for trusting her. The others felt a familiar icy calm that resembled joy. Peril had become their pastime now.

"I suppose we'd better decide what to do," said Jason.

"We'll kill it," said Pollux. "What is there to decide?"

"I think you'll have to attack it with your fists, Pollux, try to crush its head," said Jason.

"Just what I think," said Pollux.

"The problem is it won't lie still and let you do it. I think that you, Castor, should try to hold its head still, and give your brother a chance to do some punching."

"Right," said Castor.

"Another thing to consider," said Jason. "Its loop forms a circle, its head near its tail. And that tail is a weapon, too—a flail that can knock down trees."

"I'll work on that," said Idas. "I'll drive my spike through its tail and nail it to the ground."

"How about me?" said Rufus. "What do I do?"

"Swing your sledge, O smith. Beat on its back. Try to crack a spool of its spine. It's encased in triple leather, but you might make yourself felt. You, Autolycus, wield your sword, striking wherever you think best. As for me, I shall try my bow. No arrow can pierce that hide, but its palate would be vulnerable if I can shoot upward into its open mouth.

"I'm looking for work," said a clear voice.

"Daphnis!" cried Jason. "You're supposed to be safe among the trees."

"Our friend is lying so that there's a space between head and tail just big enough for me to slip through. Ekion is still out there trying to recover from his first sight of the beast."

"Why have you come?" asked Autolycus. "You can do nothing here."

"I feel invincible. That naiad frolic left me ready for anything. And I have an idea. If it works, we'll be able to depart unharmed and leave the monster guarding an empty shrine."

"Tell me your idea first."

"I'll sing to him. My father, Hermes, did that once. He tells a tale of loving another naiad long ago, one named Io. But she was guarded by a monster with a hundred eyes, who closed only fifty of them when it slept. So Hermes unslung his lyre and sang a sleepy song, closing those eyes one by one. The monster didn't even wake up when Hermes cut off its head. Well, I have a sleepy song, too."

"Start singing," said Jason.

Daphnis touched his lyre and began to sing: a song that floated strangely on the air; it did not belong to a windy night and dark deeds. It was an afternoon song, a summer song. The drowse of cicadas was in his song, the lilt of waters, and all the multitudinous tiny sounds that linger in the hush of such an hour.

Serpents' eyes have no lids and so cannot close. You can tell they are asleep only by a milky haze that covers the eyes like ashes sifting over a banked fire. Lightly, lightly, Jason stepped toward the serpent's head to see if its eyes were growing hazy. He did see its jaws gaping in a great yawn. They closed. Its tail twitched gently. Jason was hoping it would uncoil.

It did. Its tail moved away from its head. The Argonauts rushed through the open space and into the grove. They hid behind trees, watching. They were waiting for the serpent to clear the entrance to the temple so that they might return for the Fleece.

It moved away from the temple and slowly coiled itself in the center of the clearing, but in a tight bundle of loops, until it was a tall cylinder of loops, with its head on top. It lay motionless. Jason darted out; the others followed. Silently they ran past the sleeping serpent, through the brass door, into the shrine. They knelt before the glowing Fleece. It did have a power, they knew, a power that bent the strong joints of their knees. They knelt there and thanked the gods for having brought them this far.

Autolycus was the first up. He sprang to the altar, snatched the Fleece from the wall, and rolled it up. They rushed out of the temple, laughing, and ran across the clearing toward the woods. But they had laughed too soon.

Medea was in those woods. She had come back with the serpent so that she might watch it do her work of vengeance. She had rejoiced when she saw the beast encircling her enemies. She had listened in disbelief as Daphnis sang his sleepy song. Oh, how she wished she had wings to match her talons and could swoop down to seize the minstrel in her claws, silencing his song forever. But she could only listen and watch, boiling with thwarted rage, as the serpent fell asleep. Now they had the Fleece, they would race to wherever their ship was hidden and sail away, leaving her to drink her own bile forever.

It could not be; it must not be. She raised her voice in one desperate falcon shriek. That wild call stabbed the night air, freezing Jason's blood as he ran and piercing through the fog of sleep to the brain of the serpent. The beast awoke. The young men saw the moon blotted as the serpent reared above them, jaws agape.

They scattered. They were nimble. They kept dodging as the head struck at them. They merged with the shadows and flashed out, striking at the beast. But suddenly it flipped itself into the air, reshuffling its coils, feinting with its head at Jason. As he ducked away, it struck with its tail and landed a glancing blow, breaking three ribs.

Daphnis was near. He stooped to help Jason, felt a gale of foul breath, and saw the open jaws plunging down at him. They didn't touch him. Rufus was there, swinging his sledge with all the strength of his blacksmith muscles. The heavy iron peen struck the serpent's face and shattered. And those jaws swerved toward Rufus. Now Pollux did something that amazed even these brave men.

He hurled Rufus aside with a sweep of his arm and leaped into the jaws of the beast. He stood inside the lower jaw, left arm upraised, pressing the palm of his metal hand against the roof of the serpent's mouth. He stood there rigid, holding those jaws propped open and swinging his right arm with enormous force, smashing the iron maul of his fist against the serpent's teeth, knocking them out in a shower of blood and ivory.

Castor had hurled himself on the beast and had actually succeeded in looping its tail about a tree and tying a great knot. But the agonized threshing of the beast uprooted the tree, and now its flailing tail held a giant club. The tree fell on the roof of the temple, which collapsed.

Then Idas sprang in, stabbing with his spike just above the knot, stabbing so deeply that he was burying the spike up to his wrist.

Pollux, having knocked out all the teeth, began striking upward.

His iron fist crashed against the roof of the serpent's mouth—the weakest spot in its body, as Jason had said. The fist broke through the thin plate of bone, sending splinters of bone into the tiny brain. It died in a final spasm that sent Idas flying. He crashed heavily, breaking his shoulder. The same death throe had lifted Castor and smashed him to the ground, shattering his knee. Pollux staggered out of the jaws, covered with blood; particles of bone were in his hair. He swooned. Jason, pinned to the ground by the pain of broken ribs, was muttering, "Medea . . . Medea . . . let slip the beast and hunts us still."

He pulled himself to a sitting position and looked at his friends, who lay on the grass. Every breath hurt. He couldn't even pull himself up to see if anyone was alive. He tried to rise and swooned again.

Medea came out of the woods, flanked by spearmen, like a huntress with a pack of hounds. She shrieked again as she saw the fallen Argonauts. "Take them alive," she said. "But guard them well."

T W E N T Y - N I N E

E K I O N

I HAD BEEN WATCHING ALL THIS from my perch in the tree. I waited until the last clink of the patrol had died before I came down.

The serpent's corpse made a bulky shadow. I investigated splinters of moonlight and found that they were a pile of teeth, glimmering like little ivory daggers. I stumbled on something. It was the Fleece, rolled up—dropped by Autolycus and overlooked by Medea and the soldiers.

My shipmates were gone. Jason's wife had taken them to torture and death. Would they be hunting me also? I didn't want to think about that. I didn't know what to think about. Too much had happened too fast; now everything had come to a stop.

"Father, help me," I whispered.

My staff twitched in my hand. The wooden head spoke:

"Set blade to earth and dig beneath
Planting there the serpent's teeth."

Why would he want me to do that? A disagreeable prospect. I picked up a sword and poked its point into the earth to make a hole.

I walked across the field making a neat row of holes, then began another row, until I had a hundred and fifty holes. I went to the pile of ivory and took a handful. Slowly I went from hole to hole, planting a tooth in each, covering it, and lightly tamping the earth. By dawn I had sowed a hundred teeth.

I had no time to plant the rest. Before my astounded eyes, metal spikes pushed out of the earth. As I watched, a hundred armed men grew swiftly from the holes and stepped out on the field. Each man wore a helmet, breastplate, and shin greaves, wore a shield on his arm and a dagger at his belt, and carried a double-headed battle-ax. Huge, ferocious-looking men. They glared about suspiciously, not knowing where they were. I crouched behind a tree, watching.

They were blank-faced, boiling with energy. They prowled about, shouldering one another. They paired off and began to fence with their axes, dealing blows that would have smashed an ordinary warrior to the ground; easily parried such blows; and broke off to fight with someone else. Ax clanged on shield. Men grunted, snarled, bellowed, made every sound except speech. They used their axes and daggers, not as men use weapons, not as specialized tools, but as a bull uses its horns, a tiger its claws—with utter naturalness and complete ferocity.

Should I show myself? Would I last a second? Why wasn't I melting into the underbrush and slithering away? I couldn't. I wanted to, but I could not.

These men had a claim on me. Serpent seed and self-harvested they were, but it was I who had planted them and had been instructed to do so by my oracular staff. Once again I should have to imitate courage.

I stepped out from behind the tree and leaped upon a rock. "Silence!" I shouted.

All sound stopped. The men stood stock still. Every head swung toward me. The attention was total; it bristled with ferocious expectation. I understood that they had instantly, instinctively, accepted me as their leader and were awaiting orders. Their expectation robbed me of speech. No man spoke. No man moved.

"Perfect soldiers," I thought. "Sprung from monster teeth, the ultimate weapon; planted in a battlefield, never knowing the shelter of a womb, nor the nurture of breasts, but born full-grown, untouched by tenderness. How they regard me, their eyes so fixed and blank. They are like the members of a single monstrous body and I—I— have been elected brain. They're waiting for me, and I have nothing to say."

They stood in shining rows, waiting. The only movement was the plumes of their helmets bending to the small wind.

"How long will they wait? I shall have to begin. Perhaps, as I hear myself speak, I'll learn what I want to say." I raised my voice. "Hear this. We march immediately. We go to seek the enemy wherever he may be found. We do not halt night or day but march until we find him."

They shouted and beat their shields with their ax hafts. I raised my hand and they fell silent.

"Four of you fell saplings. Make a frame, weave it with boughs to make a litter for me. Cover it with that sheepskin. Two of you shall be litter bearers; detail to change every four hours. Move!"

The ranks broke. The men busied themselves. A group of six broke off and formed a circle about me, facing outward. I walked away. The circle moved with me.

"My bodyguards," I thought. "They will accompany me everywhere, allow no one to approach with hostile intent—or, perhaps, any intent. Makes one feel cared for, though it might become irksome. Perhaps not."

I mounted my litter and immediately went to sleep. I don't know how long I slept, but, awaking, knew we had come to a coastal plain.

A strong wind blew against the line of march, freighted with the smell of the sea. And the men had changed. Their regular swinging tread had become a lope. Their faces had lost their blankness, were blazing now with wild eagerness. They reminded me of a pack of hunting dogs scenting their prey.

I stood on my litter. We were moving across a great meadow. The sea glimmered in the distance. There was a brightness. I saw points of fire and heard a far sound of voices carried on the wind and a music of distant metal. Then I saw what had excited my men. An army faced them. Those were spearpoints catching the sun, armor chiming. Suddenly, with one giant voice, the men began to shout, a great clamorous yell, savage, exultant. For the first time I perceived them as human beings. For this cry was hot-blooded, spontaneous, throbbing with the terrible joy of men doing for the first time what they had been born to do.

They were killers, incredibly skilled. They fanned out, moving so swiftly that they were a blur of brass. Vastly outnumbered, they proceeded to reduce the odds. They swung out, pivoted upon themselves, cut off a forward group of the enemy, drove them into a pocket of meadow formed by an angle of bay, and hemmed them in with a hedge of iron. My men looked nothing like those they faced. Their faces were meat-red, set with eyes pale as stones; their hair was the color of brass, seeming an extension of their helmets. And they were much larger—their forearms were thicker than the Colchians' legs.

The axes rose and fell, the heavy blades shearing through shield, helmet, skull. The Colchians screamed like cattle under the butcher's sledge. Metal rang on metal. As soon as one group was slaughtered, the serpent-men swung out and corralled another group, and systematically slaughtered them. I was watching from my litter, unable to endure the massacre, uncertain about stopping it, and had slipped into a protective coma. Finally I roused myself.

"Stop!" I shouted.

Too late. The Colchians were a pile of corpses. My men were simply rooting among the pile, trying to find someone alive, using their knives to cut throats. They ceased at my shout and stood to attention.

I walked upon the field to see if I could find anyone alive. A figure scurried out from under a pile of bodies and began to run. He was immediately caught.

"Don't hurt him," I called.

He fell to his knees. "Spare my life. I was but following my leader."

"Aye, such guiltless obedience has caused more deaths than the worst intentions. I may spare your life, but I need some information."

"Gladly—anything I know."

"What happened to Prince Jason and the other Argonauts?"

"I know! Yes, I do, thank the gods! They are alive, but awaiting death."

"Do you know where they are imprisoned?"

"I can lead you right to them, merciful one."

The men were leaning on their axes, casting tall shadows. Their hands were bloody. Blood spattered their bulging forearms. Their faces were in shadow. I raised my voice.

"Men, I thank you, and seek volunteers for a special mission: twenty of you to deliver my friends from a dungeon somewhere."

Every man stepped forward.

"Again, my thanks. You make me proud to have been your leader. But I need only twenty and shall pick at random. This rank—number yourselves off, every second man, until you count to twenty. These shall come with me. The rest of you must go back whence you came and build a city there. Its site shall be the ring of trampled grass where the body of the serpent lies. I don't know the source of this mandate, but a city must rise. After that, all Colchis shall be yours. And since to hold this land is to invite invasion, you shall enjoy constant warfare."

One man shouted, "Come back and be our king!" Others took up the cry. "Come back and be our king!"

"Once more I thank you," I said. "But I don't think I'm meant for a throne. However, I have some regal friends—savage brawlers, too; you'd like them."

The men beat their ax hafts against their shields and shouted, "Ekion! Ekion! Ekion!" I hadn't realized that the syllables of my name could ring like brass.

"One by one I'm getting things I didn't know I wanted," I thought. And felt my heart swell with puzzled pride.

T H I R T Y

MEDEA STOOD ON THE BEACH gazing out to sea, and her eyes were pits of yellow fire. The sea—it was a barrier to her, but to her husband it was an avenue to freedom and glory. Here it was, out of an inlet on this wild shore, that his ship had slipped its mooring and sped southward bearing the Fleece. Off they had sailed, that thievish crew, taking the sacred relic that was her father's pride and her own dowry, that fabulous booty which seven generations of pirate kings had failed to take.

But now it was she who had failed. Despite all her cunning plots, her brilliant treachery, her brutal tactics, Jason had broken out of prison with his men, fought his way to where the *Argo* was hidden, and sailed away—leaving her behind to bear his child.

She struck her swollen belly. "Child . . . " she muttered. "You shall be the instrument of my vengeance. If you are a boy, I shall raise you to be an assassin and aim you at your father, whom you will have been taught to hate. If you are a girl, I shall train you in witchcraft. And you shall help me brew poisons and cast spells, and together we shall torture your father, even at a distance.

"But no!" she cried, tearing at her hair. "No . . . no! I don't want

distance. I must close with him. Rend his face with my claws. Sink my teeth into his throat."

She began to step in a circle, chanting:

"*Wind, icy wind,*
I'm as cold as you.
Wind, wind . . .
I am violent, too.
Wind, wind, rise for me,
Blow me over the Middle Sea."

A sharp breeze started, making the sand fly, stinging her face. Her black robe fluttered, her hair whipped. She laughed with joy and raised her long arms, flexing her talons as if to claw the sky.

"*Wind, wind, I need to know;*
Will you take me where I want to go?"

Something loomed upon the edge of the sea, black-caped, astounding. She had always been taller than men; now she had to look up, up. She heard a voice like the low howl of a hurricane just before it pounces.

"I am Boreas."

They stood on the icy beach confronting each other. Both were clad in black. Their capes blew and billowed. His beard blew. He was cavern-eyed, a giant. Flourishing in his bleak airs, she seemed to be growing to meet him.

"Lord of tempests, mighty one, destroyer of fleets, I greet you."

"You spoke a magic verse, calling me. There I was off another coast, preparing a fine punishment for a string of villages that had offended me—stirring up a tidal wave I was, when your song summoned me. What do you want?"

"I must cross the sea swiftly to kill my husband."

"What have I to do with your domestic arrangements?"

"I have read certain signs that tell me you also hate the man that I hate. He is Jason the Argonaut."

"When do you wish to leave?"

"You'll take me?"

"Climb on my back and hold on tight."

"Thank you, O stormy one, but I'm not quite ready yet. I need a few days to kill someone here, then I'll be ready to go."

"Is it Lethe, the naiad, you wish to kill?"

"How do you know that?"

"Because she it is who stole Jason from you. I know . . . I know. I watched her doing it. I wanted her, too, but she preferred that puny thief. So my love has turned to hate also."

"Then you will rejoice when she is dead, will you not? And that will be my fee to you for taking me across the sea."

"I can do my own killing," he growled. "How do you intend to catch her?"

"I have vast resources. I am a king's daughter and Hecate's priestess."

"Ridiculous! You don't have a chance of capturing her. No one takes a naiad who doesn't want to be taken. Gods, enamored, have cast wide nets and caught only fish. A certain king of Lydia, driven mad by desire, seined all the rivers, drained the lakes, blocked up the fountains—and all he caught was a chuckle she had bequeathed the waters."

"If you hate her, too, kill her for me."

"I'll kill her for myself."

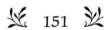

"How?"

"I haven't decided. I can blow her lake out of its bed and roll rocks over her as she flees. Or perhaps I'll sport with her a bit, for she is playful and bold. Offer to take her riding, invite her to step off a hill onto my shoulders as I fly past. Fly high, high, over sharp-pointed rocks, then simply shake her off. Naiads are very hard to kill, but that should do it."

"When will this happen?"

"Soon . . . soon."

"Then, when that is done, you shall take me to Iolcus so that I may dispatch my husband to his paramour in Tartarus."

"Farewell until I return."

The wind of his going bent the waves backward and shook the treetops.

THIRTY-ONE

IT IS SAID THAT PELIUS turned purple when he heard that Jason had fought his way through chapters of monsters, had defeated the Colchian army, and was sailing home with the Fleece. His eyes bulged like grapes, his neck ballooned, all of him darkened and swelled until he simply burst. It took seven slaves working seven days and seven nights to scrub gobbets of king off the palace walls.

But there were no welcoming crowds when Jason returned to Iolcus. For the land now was stricken with drought. No rain had fallen that year, the rivers had dried, crops had withered in the field. The animals that did not die of thirst died of hunger, and people began to starve. The sea shrank back from its shore, leaving shoals of gasping fish on a sea bottom that had become loathsome beach.

Those people who did see Jason could take no hope from the sight of him. He looked as thin as any starving farmer. He walked as though in pain. His eyes glimmered like marsh water in his sunken face. But he was king now, everyone knew. He spoke very softly but with utter authority.

He did not go to the palace. He climbed to the old temple of Thundering Zeus, which was on a hill overlooking the sea. There was a

 153

stone ledge there, a kind of natural throne. Jason donned the Golden Fleece. He wore no crown, only a chaplet of roses that Lethe had woven for him and that had never died.

People were flocking to the plain now. He raised his arms and spoke to the sky.

"O great Zeus, king of the gods, whose rod is lightning, whose footfall is thunder, you who bestow and deny at your pleasure—you, O lord, turn generous again, I beseech. Send us rain to feed our crops that we may feed our children. By this pelt that was stolen from your image and that I journeyed halfway across the world to reclaim, in the sign of this Golden Fleece, I pray, lend me the power of the Ram, the power to call rain out of the dry sky."

The people on the plain searched the sky but saw no clouds. They despaired. Strangely then, a clef of pale fire stood upon the sky, hooked down, and touched one of the temple trees with flame.

"Yes . . . yes . . . you have heard," cried Jason. "By this burning tree, answer, answer, answer with rain!"

A faint thunder growled. The sky darkened so swiftly it was as if night had been hurled upon the earth. What fell then was not rain as they had known it, but was as if Zeus, enraged by prayer, had simply lifted a lake in each hand and hurled them down upon the earth. The very fountains of heaven were broken and spilled upon the earth.

It drank thirstily, steamed, spouted, put out green banners of joy. The rivers filled. The sea returned. Jason limped down from the hill like a drowned rat. Mobs of soaked, happy people were in the roads and the streets now, frantic to adore him. But he avoided them all and shut himself up in his chamber, giving orders that no one should be admitted.

Now that he had done what he'd had to do, he felt that he had lost everything in the doing of it. His heart was sick within him, and he didn't know how to continue living. For Lethe was gone. The one creature he had loved on earth, the forgetful nymph, had again forgotten. She alone had been able to heal the ugly wound left by Medea. She had drained him of that foulness, taught him to breathe again, taught him to love. And then, at the moment of his greatest triumph, had vanished.

"It is unkingly to grieve," he said to himself. "I owe my people a brave face, a cheerful face, no matter what my loss. And perhaps, perhaps I shall see her again. No matter how forgetful she is, she may remember me. At least, I must try to believe so."

THIRTY-TWO

BOREAS CAME AGAIN TO MEDEA. He would not answer her questions, but she knew he had killed Lethe, and she rejoiced. She stepped off a hill onto his back and was whisked across the Middle Sea. They landed on the northeast shore of Iolcus, near where the *Argo* had been launched three years before.

"Before we part," said Boreas, "may I offer you some advice?"

"There is no one, dear Boreas, whom I venerate as I do you, not on earth, or in heaven, or in hell. I love and admire everything about you. Your opinion is sacred to me."

"Then hearken: if you wish to avenge yourself on Jason, drop the idea of murder. Death is too easy. His shade, released, will bound happily down to Tartarus and embrace the shade of Lethe."

"How, then, shall I punish him?"

"Let him live and live with him. You shall be a wife rejoining her husband, ready to forgive all—but forgetting nothing. And you will know how to torment him in a thousand ways."

"Will he take me back? He left me once."

"He was a pirate then. He is a king now and bound by sacred law. You are his rightful wife—a king's daughter, who will inherit a rich realm. Moreover, you are about to bear his child. He will not cast you off."

"I shall enjoy tormenting him, of course. But I hoped to marry you, you know."

"I know. And perhaps you will, but not yet. He won't last too long under your tender care."

"Will you marry me when I'm a widow?"

"We'll discuss it then."

So Medea joined Jason in Iolcus and prepared to bear her child. But then she had an idea that made her smile for the first time since leaving Boreas.

"I know how to do it," she whispered to herself. "A man like Jason, fearless, hardened by battle, made proud by victory, can only be hurt by something he loves. Witness his grief at the loss of Lethe. So I'll give him the same grief twice over and grind his soul between two millstones. By witchcraft shall I give this child, who is to be born tonight, the face and form of Lethe—her voice, her laughter, and her accursed joyousness. I can do it. That face is printed on my mind in lines of fire; they burn down to my womb and will brand that likeness on the child within. This girl who is to come tonight shall be another Lethe for him, a child he shall adore. Yes, the hooks of love will anchor themselves in that stony heart, and when the child is taken from him, the heart will be torn from his bosom. That will be my vengeance. Yes . . . yes."

That night she bore a child. A girl. Sleek and fair, with huge velvety black eyes and a nimbus of daffodil hair. When Jason bent to her in wonder, she did not cry but made a sound like the chuckling of water as it purls over rocks, and he felt an airy spear of joy piercing his chest.

For the next five years, Medea forced herself to wait patiently, but her eyes smoldered as she watched her husband and her daughter. For the girl became his shadow; she followed him everywhere, and her laughter filled the castle. She went sailing with him, riding, rock-climbing. And she went with him on sadder errands. For, as king, he cultivated his healing powers and visited the sick and the dying. He let her come with him, for he knew that the sight of her joyous face and the sound of her voice were health itself. In time to come, he thought, she would grow up to be a healer, magically endowed; already the snowdrop touch of her fingers seemed to banish pain.

But she was not to grow up. One night of wind, she vanished from her bed, and Jason led a frantic search for her. She was found by fishermen as they spread their nets the next morning. Her crushed body lay among the rocks at the foot of a cliff.

Medea vanished also. Some said that grief over her lost child had driven her to drown herself. But Jason thought otherwise. He climbed the cliff so that he could jump off and land among the same rocks that had killed his daughter. A voice spoke out of the sky. "No!"

"Why not?"

"You are king."

"Shall I be denied that which the lowliest of my subjects may have for the asking?"

"You are king—with every privilege except making yourself less."

"I don't want to live."

"You have done many things you didn't want to do and shall do more. You are a leader, god-gifted. You must serve your people, accept your loss, endure your suffering, and serve them still. You must rule them, lead them against their enemies, make laws, make rain."

Jason climbed down the cliff and went to the castle.

THIRTY-THREE

THE MYSTERY OF MEDEA made rumor sprout like weeds and grow to legend. In one story that spread throughout the lands of the Middle Sea, she prayed to Hecate to give her wings to match her claws and work to match her talents. And the arch-hag, who had long been pleased with Medea, made her an honorary harpy, conferring wings and immortality upon her. And she proved so good at her work that she became a favorite of Hades and perches on his great wrist, wings folded, waiting for him to cast her like a falcon at runaway shades. She soars high, then plunges, shrieking, freezing the shade in place, and seizes him in her talons. But she does not rend him, for he is bloodless; but bears her victim back to Hades, who decrees new torments.

What happened to Jason's crew? During their quest for the Fleece, the Argonauts had become addicted to peril and could not bear to leave each other. So they voyaged together, searching the world for promising wars, thrusting themselves always into the hottest part of the battle. Idas and the Twins managed to get themselves killed on the same afternoon. They took on an entire regiment and killed half of them before being destroyed themselves. The three shades slipped out of their ruined carcasses and swaggered down to Tartarus, vowing to fight harpies, turnspit demons, and all the legions of hell.

Rufus followed them shortly, but did not stay in Tartarus. The fires there were not for making things; they were the unproductive ovens of torment, and he refused to fuel them. He prayed to Hephaestus, asking for a transfer. Now he works in the smith-god's own smithy, which is a crater in an old Sicilian volcano named Aetna.

As for Autolycus, he did not seek death. He sought vengeance and tracks the North Wind ceaselessly. You can see him sometimes in his gray cloak, riding high, following the storm.

What happened to Daphnis? He lasted longer than most. He had formed a quenchless taste for naiads and, after writing a song, would search the waterways of the world for someone to sing it to. Finally, sun-dazed on a strange river, he tried to serenade a crocodile.

As for Ekion—he disappeared into the mists of legend. Some say he still tinkers with dreams, visiting the sleep of storytellers, planting lies that flower into truth.

When Lethe came to Tartarus she lit up the dark vaults. A fountain burst out of the ground near her garden gate. And this fountain became a blessing to the newly dead. Lethe bathed in its waters and lent them forgetfulness, so that when the newly arrived shades, exhausted by their journey, bewildered by the loss of their bodies, came to this fountain and drank its waters, they drank oblivion. They forgot who they had been when alive, forgot those they had left behind, forgot everything that would cause them pain in this place, and so were able to accept death without rancor or rebellion.

Jason's beloved child, who looked enough like Lethe to be her daughter, helps the nymph tend the fountain. And they both wait for Jason, who, they know, will join them after death and abide with them at the fountain of healing waters.

A NOTE FROM THE AUTHOR

Storytellers were telling their stories long before they knew how to write them down. Those antique wonder-tales we call myths were spoken or chanted by warrior minstrels who wandered the dangerous roads from castle to castle and campfire to campfire, singing for their supper. Full of murder and marvels and mystery was the crude verse chanted by these bards—songs of heroes, gods, and monsters; of cattle raids, piracy, elopements; of battles fought for the love of a woman and won or lost by the whim of a god.

Some stories grew to be favorites and were told over and over again, and each bard telling the same tale told it differently. But all this time a written language was slowly growing, permitting some learned minstrels to commit their story-songs to those marks which could magically transform themselves into living words. And each time the same story was written down by someone else, something changed.

A blind bard named Homer, for example, gathered hundreds of tales about a war that had been fought five hundred years before and

about the voyage home of a war-chief called Ulysses and wove them into two mighty epics, the *Iliad* and the *Odyssey*. And his stories differed from all that had gone before. The old, old tales had passed through the fire of his genius and had been changed forever.

A word now about this book, which differs so from other accounts of Jason, Medea, and the Argonauts.

The cycle of tales that make up the Argosy are among the earliest in Greek mythology. As has been seen, there is no "authorized text" of any myth, and particularly none of this cycle, which varies wildly in all its versions. Fragments lodge in the work of Pindar, Hesiod, Appolodorus, Apollonius Rhodius, Homer, and Herodotus, and of a later Roman author named Valerius Flaccus—much of it untranslated and accessible only to those who read Greek and Latin. Having undergone the privileged ordeal of a classical education, I have been able to pick and choose among those bits and pieces and half-told tales, and use those people and events which best suit my own way of telling a story.

But why is the source material of the Argosy more confused and formless than other myth-cycles? Well, there is considerable evidence that the reports of this voyage were engendered by not one but *several* quests for a Golden Fleece, or other sacred relic, stolen by Black Sea raiders from some coastal temple on the Peloponnese. Seven generations of pirate kings from the lands of Hellas recruited warrior crews and sailed across the Middle Sea to recapture the magic loot. Seven voyages—at least—spanned some two hundred years, all happening about four thousand years ago. The stories intermingle, the routes intertwine; islands pop up and sink away, place names and people names jostle and obscure one another. And each mythographer must find his own way through the fabulous rubble and recast the tale according to his own vision.

163

About Medea: like many names this was a word first, then a title, finally a given name. Originally, "Medea" simply meant "clever," but as time passed it gathered darkness and came to mean "weirdly clever," being especially used to described women who did magic— very much like our word "witch," whose first meaning was "sharp-witted," or wise. So by the time the *Argo* sailed, "Medea" meant "witch" in that language, and was considered too unlucky a word to use unless you had to. For magic bubbled closer to the surface then, and witches were much feared. Among other charming habits they were known to eat babies.

Actually, the legend of a woman named Medea began long before the first Argosy began and lingered long after the last one ended, and sprouted into many forms. In later tales she is also depicted as being the wife of Aegeus, making her the stepmother of Theseus. In another account she comes to Attica simply to kill Aegeus, seeks to kill Theseus, and vanishes. She appears in still another group of linked stories as a cruel sorceress queen of Corinth, slain finally by her subjects when her crimes became too much to stomach.

The Athenian playwright Euripides, writing some fifteen hundred years after Medea did or did not do the things she was accused of, adapted one tale to his own purpose, and it became the play *Medea*. This drama shows her being driven mad by jealousy because Jason has decided to cast her aside and marry a richer younger princess. Her madness culminates in murder when she butchers their two children.

This is what she became best known for, but is not what I would choose to emphasize.

A tale well told is a kind of Argosy, launching you on uncharted seas and taking you among perils and pleasures that are very strange but half-familiar as if fledged out of your own dreams. Is it a coincidence that the oldest words for ship and book are the same—the word "bark"?

Among my happiest memories are those when I felt myself embarking on such a voyage of joyous piracy, knowing the vaults of my imagination were filling with a treasure that would out-glitter gold.